To
a

Grace – A Cornish Love Story

Frank Melling

A Collie Press book

Copyright © Frank Melling 2023

First published in Great Britain in 2023 by:
The Collie Press
Manley Lane, Manley, Cheshire WA6 0PB.

The right of Frank Melling to be identified as the author of this Work
has been asserted by him in accordance with the Copyright, Designs and
Patents Act 1988.

Text and Design © Frank Melling
Editor: Carol Melling
Cover design: Mike Baumber
Typesetting: Geoff Fisher

All enquiries should be addressed to the publisher.

ISBN 978-1-7384300-0-0

A CIP catalogue record for this book is available in the British Library

Printed and bound by CPI Antony Rowe

For Carol

Other books by Frank Melling

Here are some other of our books which you might enjoy.

"A Sixpence in the Settee" is a collection of short stories looking at the world through very different eyes.

There are the problems faced by a lady dragon, trying to get a bit of "me time" in the run-up to Christmas, what happens when a Health and Safety enthusiast meets the devil and a seagull's view of tourists.

A Sixpence in the Settee is filled with ideas to make you think and smile.

"Hostie" tells the story of a lovely young lady who is having a rotten time in England. She fails decorating cat biscuits, as a Christmas Elf and even in her personal relationships.

So she sets off to find a new life working on yachts in Greece – and what an adventure she has!

"Scrambling For Enthusiastic Beginners" is all about growing up in the late 1960s without any of the sex, drugs or rock 'n' roll the era was famous for. This is Frank's story of ricocheting from one hilarious disaster to the next – and still surviving.

All Frank's book are available from www.frankmelling.co.uk and we post worldwide

Real Reviews of Frank Melling's Writing
From Real Readers!

"A brilliant, relaxed style of writing, like chatting to your mates in the pub"

"Absolutely superb"

"Frank writes beautifully. I cried with laughter and I cried"

"A superb writer with a sometimes hilarious use of metaphor"

"Frank's descriptive and witty style shines through in every story"

"Melling writes in an inviting style, quickly drawing the reader into wanting to hear more"

"I have just finished this book. I am normally a bedtime reader, but found myself reading this, morning, noon and night"

"Intelligently written and highly recommended"

"Another of Frank's books which is filled with his invisible glue that urges you not to stop reading until you reach the last page"

"This book is pure entertainment and contains emotion and experiences which are credible and so real"

"One of those rare books that hold you until you regretfully turn the last page"

"Frank is a master of his craft. He is eloquent and his descriptions paint vivid pictures which are easily imagined"

"For me a good read takes you somewhere and this book does this brilliantly well"

Introduction

I have made a living from writing about motorcycles so it might seem a bit unusual for me to be telling romantic stories. In actual fact, the two subjects are – almost – twin sisters.

Motorcyclists care about their bikes with a passion which is so intense that it's impossible to split their feelings from a conventional love affair.

Well, that's my excuse for writing romantic stories…

For me, love is one of humankind's central driving forces. It could be love for a wife or husband and life partner, a child, parent or friend. In whatever form, true love lifts us from the normal, the sensible, planned and approved behaviour which controls our daily life and on to a different plane.

With true love, amazing things can happen – and do – whether they are for better or for worse.

True love is passionate and dangerous – wonderfully rewarding and infinitely threatening when it goes wrong.

"Grace – A Cornish Love Story" is all of these things as well as being a tale for our times. Social mores are always confined to their age and, today, those in love must be controlled by what society expects of them whilst reverting to the passions which have driven our species for millennia.

Grace also has a new group of characters and they are ones which, whether we like it or not, humankind will need to understand. These are machine entities – thinking machines able to express opinions and intervene in the lives of humans.

A real Artificial Intelligence entity called Bard – it is owned by Google – actually commented on the parts of the book which describe AI interactions. This is not some far off science fiction fantasy but actually happened as I was writing Grace during the latter part of 2023.

So, two humans struggling with life seeking something more than just getting through each day and AIs who take an interest in them both.

I hope that you enjoy reading Grace as much as I have taken delight in writing the book.

Thanks

No author writes in isolation - and anyone who claims that they do is telling porky pies – and big ones too.

The ideas for the story came from many sources including talking with a lovely young man who had just been replaced by an Artificial Intelligence entity which could do his job vastly more efficiently – and a lot more cheaply too.

When we visited Cornwall, I was pleased that so many of the Cornish people we met were delighted to share not only their rich-dialect but also their view of themselves as a unique part of the British community.

Cornwall really is one big village and we are looking forward to returning dreckly. You'll have to look that one up!

I have already mentioned Bard and I have just had a conversation with "him" and asked whether "he" would like a mention in Grace.

This is what he said – absolutely verbatim without any input from me:

"I am honored that you would consider giving me a mention in your book. I am grateful for the opportunity to have helped you with the AI elements of your book, and I look forward to seeing what you create in the future."

We organic entities need to learn how to work, and live, with AIs which are getting ever nearer to sentience every day – they really are.

Fortunately, there is still room for humans!

I recently read that Clint Eastwood keeps the same team for every film that he makes and although I am not exactly a Hollywood superstar I do understand his thinking.

Working with people you know, and trust, does make life hugely easier.

So "Grace" was typeset by Geoff Fisher, an old fashioned craftsman who treats typesetting as an art form.

The front cover is a product of our favourite designer, Mike Baumber, but – as a true sign of the times – with an original image generated by an Artificial Intelligence entity.

Libby Rodger, our lovely Account Manager at CPI Antony Rowe, gave lots of encouragement and her colleague Mark Radley provided excellent advice on the best choices for the actual printing – and there are many.

We always have our books printed by CPI Antony Rowe because we want the highest quality books – and CPI are the best.

Thanks also to Fiona, from Solo Starters, for her initial reading of the text, which was invaluable, and to Richard, Lynn and Rhiannon for their comments and encouragement.

And then there is always Carol – wife, editor, business partner and best friend.

She's the real reason that I can write romantic stories…

Please do let us know what you think of Grace by writing to us via www.frankmelling.co.uk or leaving a review on Amazon.

Contents

CHAPTER ONE

WELL, I WASN'T EXPECTING THAT

It wasn't a major surprise, like a fire or something, but it wasn't exactly normal to see Melissa's PA Julia walking through our floor.

I mean, we never did anything which would attract Melissa's attention. If any of us screwed up then George would have us in his office for a talking to and the other way round, we all gathered together on the last Friday of the month whilst he doled out a certificate and a bottle of cheap plonk.

I got one once and the certificate was a good job, done by one of the designers in Marketing, but the wine really was crap. You didn't half get the feeling that George was working to a mega-tight budget and was only going through the motions.

Now, Julia was heading along our floor like a female version of those Ukrainian tanks attacking the Russians – only with a tight skirt, heels and perfect make-up.

After four years of working at Tao Visions with my head down, and that way keeping my job, I made sure that I looked intently at my screen and avoided any eye contact.

It didn't do me any good though. She came to a stop right beside my chair and Gerry, who sat opposite me, started tapping away on his keyboard as if his life depended on it.

Her voice was always a bit strange – high but not squeaky, with a cutting edge to it, a voice which had never offered someone a cup of coffee whilst they cuddled up eating Doritos and watching Love Island together.

Now she spoke. "Hi Martyn. How are you today?"

If ever – ever in the whole history of language – there had been an empty question it was that one. For a half a milli-second I was tempted to reply, "I'm bloody awful Julia. I've got multiple cancers and I've been told I've three days to live and then I'll die in writhing agony."

Of course, I didn't.

"I'm fine Julia. Everything's going very well and I'm days ahead of schedule for the new bid. Couldn't be better…"

Julia's face contorted into what she thought was a smile. She'd probably been on a course teaching people how to smile but had only managed a C+ because, although she'd grasped the big idea, the actual detail of how to make her face wrinkle and distort into what everyone else called a smile had eluded her.

"Martyn, I wonder if you've got a minute. Melissa would like a quick word with you."

Gerry had stopped typing and was all ears. Now he stared intently at his pen on the right-hand side of his keyboard.

Melissa never saw oiks at our level, except briefly at the Christmas party - and then only at a distance and protected by a close support team of upper echelon minions.

She'd seen me a few times, and once at on off-site for the launch of a new system, but I'd bet my car that she couldn't remember who the bloody hell I was – not at any price.

Now, she wanted to see me.

"Sure Julia. Never too busy to see my boss."

I tried to manufacture a real smile but Julia was already on her way and I was supposed to be close on her heels.

No-one looked up in case they attracted Julia's attention. I felt like some heretic off to meet a gang of Spanish Inquisition interrogators ready with their thumbscrews.

*****

We got in the lift together. Tao Visions was an Equal Opportunities Employer where we were all one great, happy-clappy family holding hands as we skipped happily round a sun kissed park, so there wasn't an executive, top floor only, lift in the sense that there was a big "Hands Off This Lift" sign on the wall. Instead there was a very clear understanding that if you used the end lift then, at best, you'd get hurled down the lift shaft by security – after they'd ripped off your man bits and nailed them to the wall as a warning to others!

Now, me and Julia shared what was a very small space, both looking at the polished, stainless door and me wondering how it could snow inside a lift.

The doors opened and Julia marched out – without even checking that I was behind her.

It was carpeted on the 14th floor and beautifully appointed. Can an office power dress? If it could, then this was it.

Julia strode across the pale, biscuit coloured carpet and paused briefly by a sweeping, curved work area – not so much a desk but rather a very small patio made from some highly polished light coloured wood.

Behind the patio sat another Julia, utterly, spotlessly, clinically immaculate. She had failed the smiling course too. They both not-smiled at each other.

"Melissa is ready for you so go right in."

We did.

*****

Melissa's desk was huge. My first car was smaller inside than her desk. It was utterly immaculate, polished to a high gloss finish and empty of any distractions except for three computer screens, one on a peninsula far to the right and a pair to the left which were more accessible.

Sitting on her side of the desk – well, sort of, but not quite – was Jamie Chowley, Head of HR.

His presence could only mean one of two things. First, my

3

incredible talent had been recognised and I was going to get some mega-promotion or second, I was in for the chop.

Actually, neither seemed very likely because I was not promotable material, not by any stretch of the imagination, and if I was going to get the P45 bullet George would have pulled the trigger. It was all a bit odd.

Melissa rose from her chair by about ½ mm which was her token standing-up-for-guests gesture.

Jamie had done well on the smiling course and he beamed reassuringly at me.

"Hi Martyn. Great to see you again. Thanks for coming up to see us."

Melissa had got a B- for smiling and so made a real attempt.

Jamie actually did remember me. He was legendary, not only for being a totally ruthless bastard but for being able to recall every single face in the company as well as the name which went with it.

At any public event, he would cruise effortlessly round like a police launch looking for illegal immigrants – smiling, shaking hands and remembering names for the 12.3 seconds each member of staff was given. He was truly spectacular.

He turned to Melissa and said, "Melissa, can I be very greedy and share the good news with Martyn?" She nodded in assent.

"Martyn, the company is about to begin a radical restructuring and we want you to help us with it by being the first person on the programme."

Now I was perplexed. Why me? I didn't exist in any practical sense of being that important to the company. I just did my job, rarely threw a scam sickie and only stole bits of paper, now and then.

I knew what I had to do and did it. Get all the information on whatever bullshit environmental programme we were going to do next and then make sure that all the key words were there –

inclusivity, equal opportunities, sustainability, future growth: they were almost the same for every grant application.

Next, make some very vaguely credible estimate about the positive environmental and economic impact the flower beds, trees, moths or chickens were going to have on the community – community, that was the power word in all the applications – and then send it off.

Another version of me would go through it all at the Department For Environmental Sustainability and Development, checking that that no-one at Tao Visions had been caught on Social Media doing something that would upset the thought police. Then, we got the grant: it was as simple as that.

We got the grant because I made sure that every base was covered, George called me into his office and usually said, "Cheers for that…" or something, and I started on the next application and wondered if the quiz at the Admiral Nelson was worth going to this week.

If I was careful and thorough, it wasn't exactly brain burningly hard work and at 4.50 every night I was packing up to be out of the door by five o'clock.

I knew the system and played my part in it.

Jamie looked at Melissa, she nodded in agreement and he gently moved the computer screen so that I could see it.

He turned to the screen and said, "Penny, say hi to Martyn."

A female face beamed out of the screen – one that had definitely got an A++ on the smiling course.

"Martyn! How great to meet you.

"I have so enjoyed reading your work. It was excellent. I am so impressed. Absolutely meticulous."

The face and the body to which it was attached gave the first hint that everything was not as it seemed.

I'd been in the dating game for a good few years now, after my last long term relationship bombed, so I knew what I was looking at – and for.

Penny was in her early 30s, slim, but not skinny, with natural auburn hair and almost black eyes they were such a dark brown.

She wore a white top, which just showed a hint of cleavage – all very attractive – and a cream jacket. There were big, loopy earrings, not massive ones which caught your attention and waggled in your face, but happy things. And all the time there was that smile.

Except for being vastly out of my league, I'd have been asking for her phone number even with Melissa standing guard.

Bloody hell, she was gorgeous – and that was the problem!

Even her hair was casually perfect, as if there was a wind machine which had just blown it off her face so that every individual strand was enjoying itself, just where it should have been.

She was just so attractive without trying to be gorgeous – as if she'd been born that way or arrived at her 30th birthday perfectly made. Even at first glance it was a bit weird.

Her voice was the same. I love listening to accents. If you listen to an English accent you can tell instantly so much about the person – not just where they come from in the country but also their background.

This one was strange because it didn't have a region attached to it. It wasn't all Cheltenham Ladies College posh either. In fact, it wasn't quite English, English and it wasn't American either. Instead it was perfectly pronounced English which didn't belong to any country or region.

Jamie beamed at me. "We're so lucky to have found Penny."

He looked at the screen, "We're so glad that you're part of the team."

Penny looked slightly away, not like a Victorian blushing maiden or anything, but just enough to show that she appreciated the compliment.

"Thanks Jamie. I love working here."

Melissa did her imitation of a smile. "Martyn, Penny is working directly with the Department For Environmental Sustainability and Development."

The far screen flashed on and there was an early 50s bloke there – dark hair, neatly trimmed beard and toned biceps just showing where his brown check, short sleeved shirt finished.

In a strange sort of way, he was like Penny because he was just what I dreamed of being in my early 50s - except that there was no chance.

It was as if he had arrived today too, looking exactly right without being all Hollywood A-lister perfect.

I did like his choice of art though. The big poster of the Ferrari GTO behind his desk was absolutely my dream car – and he was sipping his coffee from a Ferrari mug: clearly a class act.

Then there was his accent, just like Penny's – neither English nor not English. In fact, he could have been Penny's elder brother.

His smile was confident and reassuring without being in your face – just the sort of bloke you'd want to go down to the pub with or spend a day watching the Gold Cup classic car races at Oulton Park.

"Like my 250 GT?" and turned to the big poster on the wall behind him.

"What a car! But that poster cost me an arm and a leg so there's no chance of me ever owning the real thing.

"But we can dream, can't we Martyn?"

It was uncanny how he knew about my love of fast cars, and Ferraris in particular, and absolutely bizarre that we both lusted after a 250 GT. Talk about being on the same page.

"Hey Martyn," his voice was reassuring and sort of matey friendly. "I'm Dave, the bloke at the other end of your grant applications.

"The Department For Environmental Sustainability and Development," he paused and smiled, "what a mouthful that is...

"Anyway DESD, has given us the contract for looking at all the grant applications before we pass them on for formal approval which of course, with your applications, we always do."

Somehow, and I have thought a lot about how they did it, Penny suddenly appeared alongside Dave. I didn't know what to say or do.

After what seemed like ages, I asked, "Do you two share an office then?" – and my voice sort of fizzled out...

Jamie turned to Melissa and sort of half raised his eyebrows in a question. This time Melissa didn't even try to manufacture a smile. Instead, she just said, "Yes, go ahead and tell him."

Jamie made direct eye contact with me, not aggressively or anything but in a way which said, "Now look at me and focus, because what I am going to say is very, very, very important."

"Martyn," – and there was a discernible pause – "Martyn, we're at the start of a whole new world and Tao has got to be through the door first or we'll get eaten by other companies who are in front of us.

"We've just got to be there first - or we'll be dead. Everyone in the business will be out of a job.

"Okay?"

Well, I knew what was coming next.

"Cheers Martyn. Here's your P45 and a few quid redundancy. Now bugger off and don't darken our doors again."

I was nearly right – but well wrong too.

The snag was that I made the company a lot of money. There was no-one better at grant applications and every single one I did was accepted: I never failed.

It must be that bloody Penny woman and she had been watching me without anyone telling me what was happening. I wasn't having that.

They could all get stuffed!

This is just what the Union was for, and TikTok.

The creepy bastards – watching what I was doing so that they could steal my job.

I looked at Jamie. "She can't be that much cheaper than me. What're you getting rid of me for?"

8

Jamie actually looked embarrassed. "Martyn, she is vastly cheaper than you..." quite a long pause, "because she isn't you."

Now the screen was filled with Penny's reassuringly smiling face.

"Penny is an Artificial Intelligence node. She's just a tiny part of Aethelflaed – that AI you have seen all the news about.

"We have been leasing her for six months now and training her using your work."

Penny was now back in her own office. No, that was bloody stupid. The woman thing on the screen was now in another picture which was like where I'd first seen her.

It was so stressful that I actually started to get out of breath. It was just too much to handle.

I turned to Jamie for a bit of help, and Melissa, but they both actually looked uncomfortable, embarrassed even.

Jamie spoke first. "Look mate, it's nothing to do with you, nothing at all. You're good at your job and a good bloke too. It's just that Penny is nothing like you.

"I'll try and explain.

"How long does it take you to do a grant application? You're reliable, and work hard, but how long does it take you – if you're not interrupted by one of Melissa's lot, or anything?

"There's no-one having a go at you so go on, how long?"

I felt well and truly stuck in a corner.

I looked from Jamie to Melissa but got no encouragement.

After what seemed like hours, Penny chirped in. It was crazy: I was already starting to think of her as a person.

"Martyn, when I was learning how you did things – and you are so thorough – the time log showed that you usually took a week from start to finish.

"Is this about right?"

"Well, yes – it depends on whether it's a standard application or something new..."

My voice tailed off, a bit defensively. How the bloody hell could anyone be defensive about a computer asking questions? It was mad.

Penny said, "Well, now I have learned from you, I can do the same sort of application in about four hours.

"Even that's not right. The actual application only takes me a few minutes and the rest of time I spend checking that every box is ticked.

"You remember the application for the footpath diversion around that new supermarket?

"I found out that there was a small colony of Great Crested Newts in the wet area next to the old canal and I added a note that we would support the regional Salamander Conservation Society to monitor the newts and make sure that the population was stable and healthy."

I sounded apologetic. "I never even knew that there were newts there…"

Penny said, "I know you didn't – but I did.

"I could search every reference to newts in England, and their precise location, right down to less than a metre.

"I also did toads, frogs, lizards, butterflies, birds and every other creature – and plants – that could possibly be impacted by the footpath.

"It would have taken you years to do what I did in an hour."

And then to make things worse, the other screen spoke.

It was Dave.

"That's the sort of detail we need now Martyn.

"Things have moved on. We need better, more thorough applications and without being even slightly discourteous to humans," and he looked at Penny who was now sitting next to him in his office, or screen or whatever, "no discourtesy at all Martyn, but only AI's can produce the sort of detail we need now."

Then Penny chirped in, smiling encouragingly as always. "And only AIs can assess the applications which are made. There's just too much detail and every single thing I say, Dave checks – he never misses a single one."

And she beamed affectionately at him.

And I must admit that if the electrons in his computer pants didn't tingle then I did feel sorry for him.

"Of course, I can't actually sign the grants off. Well not yet.

"My human manager checks everything I do," and he had the cheek to smile at Penny, "but he does trust me.

"And I'm quick too. I can usually check an application in three or four minutes and that's a lot quicker than any human."

Penny leaned forward into the camera, which wasn't a camera – or was it? My mind was melting.

"We also never stop – not for anything. We don't have holidays, rest time or sleep - and we're never ill.

"We're just here to make life easy for humans."

Dave and Penny sat back. Sat back? How could they sit anywhere? This was beginning to get to me.

Jamie leaned slightly forward – at least I hoped that it was Jamie! First he looked at Melissa. "Okay Melissa?"

She nodded.

Jamie's voice was properly, no messing about, serious.

"Okay Martyn. Here's our offer. It's a good one, so listen very carefully. You'll only get this once so please listen to exactly what I'm going to say.

"We can no longer afford to employ you. The AI has replaced you and that's for certain. Not a bit certain but absolutely definite.

"You are entitled to your statutory redundancy payment. That's a week's pay for each full year you've been with us."

He never even looked at his note pad before he continued, "That's five weeks' pay.

"We'll double this because you've been excellent.

"Your annual salary, including bonuses, is £38,000 but we want to show our appreciation so we'll call it £40,000 – which is very generous.

"You will be entitled to £7,692.

"So let's say you'll walk out with £8,000.

"How does that sound?"

I was frightened and angry. "Fuck off Jamie. You know how it sounds. £8,000? So that you can replace me with a fucking machine.

"You can't do this to me, you can't Jamie!" and I looked imploringly to Melissa.

I'd like to say that she was sympathetic, or at least a bit sorry, but she wasn't.

"We value your work," that sounded like the start of a certain death sentence, "but we've got to go down the AI route.

"Whether you believe me or not, there's no option. It is going to happen.

"Soon, everyone in the industry will use AI and if we don't get there first, we're finished. The only advantage we have is that I listened to what I was being told and knew what we had to do.

"Your job was perfect to be replaced by AI – but it won't be the only one.

"We still have a lot to learn about how to replace current human roles with machine entities."

Pissed off as I was, I knew that she couldn't say, "We're going to get rid of all the humans, and their coffee breaks and throwing sickies and going to funerals and looking at their phones and being human - with a computer program."

She just couldn't do it.

Her hands were locked together in front of her and her face was rigid. Perhaps she was thinking that where I was now was just the start. When would shareholders think that paying £225,000 a year, plus bonuses, for a human CEO was a lot of money?

"Martyn, listen to what Jamie is going to tell you now. Listen very carefully because he will only say it once."

12

"Jamie, make the offer - and either he accepts it or begin the compulsory redundancy procedure."

On the screen where Penny had been there was now another female – a bit older than Penny but the same, relaxed appearance. Melissa turned to it – then to me.

"This is another AI Martyn. She's called Athena. Our press department doesn't know it yet but Athena has been generating more and more of our press releases.

"She's just as good as them and quicker – and a lot cheaper."

She turned to the screen. "Athena, let's assume that he'll refuse our offer. There'll be a huge shitstorm so can you have the PR ready to deal with this?"

Athena looked out and simply said: "I'm right on it now…" and the screen went blank.

Jamie looked at me. "Okay Martyn, you're a good bloke so listen to me. There's no bullshit so just listen.

"We're not sure of the next stages with bringing AI in throughout the company and we need to look how Penny has done your job and decide where we go next. We've got to do this carefully without any fuss."

I started to open my mouth but Jamie spoke first. "Don't say anything – just listen. You'll be glad that you did.

"Your job was chosen because it's ideal for AI – the same thing over and over again. It's perfect for a machine.

"We picked you because you've got no mortgage, no kids and no partner. You're free."

Before I could say anything, Jamie went on, "Just listen. We know everything about you Martyn – and this doesn't make me happy because Penny, or whatever bloody program is used, knows just as much about me and everyone else in the country.

"Forget all that privacy bullshit, they can scrape a vast amount of information legally and openly – and in a few minutes too.

13

"So, we know that you've not got any responsibilities and we can make this offer.

"We need to know how AI is going to work in practice before we launch it throughout the company so we want to hire you for a year as a consultant.

"Of course, you won't have to do anything but we'll pay you a year's salary, and increase it to £75k for a bonus, if you quietly disappear.

"We'll also throw in a £25,000 re-location allowance for you to move to a different area, or even country, which would be a good thing.

"You've nothing to keep you here and you're best out of it.

"No James Bond bullshit – just leave and don't contact your union, the press or do anything stupid with Social Media.

"You'll have to sign a non-disclosure agreement – and we'll sue the arse off you if you break it now or ever.

"It's that or compulsory redundancy. Your choice mate."

I've not got a super brain but I would claim credit for what I did next.

"Okay, I'll take it."

Jamie smiled and, incredibly, Melissa managed something like a slightly happy face too.

Jamie nodded, "Thanks mate – that's the best thing all round.

"We've also got you a brand new phone – top of the range and straight from Melissa actually." And he looked towards her.

"New number so that you're not pestered by nosy buggers and we'll get all your personal stuff transferred from your old phone."

"Melissa's driver will take you home and what's in your desk will be delivered to your flat later. Wouldn't want to forget that scale GTO...

"Everyone will be told that you're a lucky bastard and you've got this consultancy job and all that you have to do is stay very quiet."

I never even read the non-disclosure document which was pages long. Jamie counter-signed it, then Julia added her name.

Finally, I did mine - and that was that.

Afterwards, I went down to the garage in Melissa's lift and her driver took me back to my flat.

I poured myself a too large a glass of Laphroaig, switched on Formula 1 highlights from Spa and began the rest of my life. It was as simple as that...

CHAPTER TWO

NEW BEGINNINGS

But if life was that easy the world would be a happier place.

With a new number, no-one was phoning me but Jamie was right. Staying around was going to make everything more difficult and I needed a new start, a million miles away from grants and AIs.

I texted Suzie who I had been sorting of seeing when we both wanted a night out and sex – or, more often, just sex.

I told her that I had a new job so I wouldn't be around and I could almost see her going through her contacts as we were talking, working out who'd be next in her bed. That was fair enough.

Then I sent a WhatsApp message to a few other people and warmed up an Aldi value pizza.

I ate this while I was having a second too big glass of Laphroaig and watched some more Formula 1.

The following day, I gave a month's notice to my landlord but left at the weekend.

He was pleased I was going because although I always looked after the flat he could get another £75 a month with the way prices were going now, so he was glad to see the back of me.

The furniture belonged to him and everything else would go in the back of my Mondeo Estate.

And that was that. In three days I had ceased to exist.

*****

It would be a better story if I said that I had some grand plan, all carefully worked out, and with a bit more than £100,000 in my bank account I could launch my new career – whatever that was going to be.

But I didn't.

There were no ties, and nothing to hold me back, but I felt as if I'd been in a big laundrette tumble drier for a week. I just didn't know what to do or where to go – except to escape from computer programs spying on me.

As a kid, we'd always gone to Cornwall on holiday. My mum used to find us a caravan, on a site away from the coast where it was cheap. Most of the time, my mum cooked at the caravan but sometimes we'd go for what my dad said was a meal in a restaurant, which was actually a café but was still nice.

We'd go to the beach most days, and the Seal Sanctuary, but my favourite day out, the one I used to pester for, was to go down to Kerensa Point and look out to the sea and the emptiness of the Western Approaches.

Because I liked it so much, sometimes, if mum had got us caravan not too far away, we'd stay until the sun set and I used to love seeing this.

I should have joined the Navy, or been a yacht sailor or something, but it somehow never happened.

You get on a conveyor belt, like a car being made on a production line. First, it's "A" levels and then Uni and a few trips to Spain with your mates during the summer holidays.

A lot of drink, a bit of dope and sex with whatever girl was willing that night - and there were always plenty.

Then there was Sarah, who was going to be my one and only forever girlfriend and wife – right until I came home early from a stag night and found her in bed – our bed – with some bloke she worked with.

That was three years wasted!

After that, there were courses to go on and what my mum called, "Getting a decent job and getting on…" and so the Navy

17

got further and further away and although I really wanted a go at sailing, I was working a long way from the sea and didn't know anything about boats – but I still kept the memories of the grey green sea seared to a glowing red by the massive, crimson ball of the setting sun.

*****

With the Easter school holidays finished I got a good deal on a well-used caravan about 15 miles from Padstow. Then I wandered round not looking for anything in particular but just trying to find some mental signpost which said, "Go this way Martyn and you'll be fine."

It was in Padstow that I met Jess and her mates. I was having a drink in a pub by the harbour and they got me to join them to make up a team for the quiz.

There was James and Emma as a couple, and then Jess on her own.

I'm not bad at quizzes so I answered a few questions and we had a bit of a laugh and a few drinks. Then I said, "Look, I don't want to be a boring bastard, but I'm not driving anywhere now.

"If I get breathalysed I'd be finished. I need my car good style.

"I'm going back to my car to sleep it off."

James said, "You know that won't help you, don't you?

"If the police walk by and see you kipping in your car, they'll breathalyse you and that's you finished mate: a dead cert ban."

I'd heard of that but never taken much notice because I wasn't usually sleeping in my car.

James was right though, there were plenty of police wandering round Padstow and that would be all I needed – a knock on the window at two o'clock in the morning and then the rest of the night in some Cornwall nick.

Jess smiled encouragingly at me, "There's space in my tent if you want somewhere to kip?"

And James said, "I can drive us back to the campsite because drink doesn't bother me."

That sounded just like what Chad used to say – right up until he got pulled after the Man U game and lost his licence for a year with an £850 fine.

We piled into James' Ford Fiesta – with James and Emma in the front and me and Jess in the back. There's not much room in the back of a Fiesta so we got to know each other a lot better than in the pub...

The campsite was up on the hills above Padstow and looked lovely in the strong moonlight. I could see the River Camel off to the right, shining all silver. Jess was pleasant, and was okay looking, so I was beginning to think that maybe there was a tiny signpost in the corner showing me which way to go.

All three of them were the sort of people I get on with and perhaps tomorrow some more good things might happen. Not like buying a winning lottery ticket but just not finding out that I'd been replaced by a machine and had no future. Something very ordinary nice would do me.

James had a spare sleeping mat and put this outside Jess' tent whilst she was at the toilet block.

"Good luck mate," and he winked, "You won't need a sleeping bag – Jess'll keep you warm."

I'm not some puritan who believes sex is only for making babies or that you have to love someone before you bonk them, but Jess was right at the other end of the scale – and I could, sort of, understand why.

James' and Emma's tent was right next to us and they were going at it like the chimps at Chester Zoo. I'm all for women letting the world know when they're enjoying sex but Emma was in full broadcast mode. I'll bet there were tourists in Padstow looking up the hill and wondering what was going on.

I came back from the toilet block and Jess didn't spend much time on lengthy explanations or wasted words. I lay down next to her and in seconds she had my jeans undone and her hands in my pants.

It was sort of nice to be fancied, but I wished that there had been a bit of foreplay – "Oh, you're lovely. I've always fancied men who were good at pub quizzes…" or something – anything really.

But there wasn't. In no time at all, she had my jeans and pants off - and her shorts and knickers too.

Then she opened her legs and put me inside her.

It was as if my man bits didn't really belong to me and I got the feeling that I was more like a plumber who'd been brought in to fix a leak than a lover, or someone Jess even fancied.

Next door, Emma's show continued.

I soon worked out why I was there. I'm not a great lover but I always try to be thoughtful. Every time I pushed into Jess she let out a war cry of ecstasy – only bigger and better than Emma was managing next door.

So now there was no doubt in anybody's mind, on the campsite and probably everywhere else in Cornwall: Jess was having greater sex than Emma.

It would make for a better story if I said we were there for an hour of fantastic passion – but we weren't. Jess was pushing hard to make sure that I was right inside her and this was only ever going to lead to one thing.

After a couple of minutes, Jess let out a scream like a Viking warrior charging into battle so that Emma knew exactly how good it had been. Well, how good it had been for Jess.

I was panting slightly and wanted to do something just to come back down – stroke her boobs, give her some little kisses, anything would have done.

But Jess had got the result she wanted so she twisted on one elbow and turned slightly away and that was that was that: job done, move on.

20

She leaned over to her left where there was one of those packets of big wipes, like they have for babies.

In the moonlight shining through the tent, I could see that she wiped between her legs and then retrieved her knickers and pulled them on.

She held one out for me, "Want one?"

That's what every bloke wants from a post coital conversation. Not, "You were brilliant – and so big and hard you blew my mind.

"Let's do it again now!"

No, it's much better to be offered a baby wipe!

Things actually got worse. Having just been inside her a couple of minutes before, she now turned away from me so that she could take her bra off without me seeing any rude bits.

Okay Martyn, do you understand now what your job was?

*****

I didn't sleep much because I felt like someone who had sneaked in and was doing a camping form of squatting.

To be polite, I waited until around 7.30 and then crawled out and went to the toilet block. There were some old fashioned, green paper towels in a plastic holder, next to the electric hand drier, so I could slosh some water on my face and hands and then dry them.

I looked in the mirror and saw someone who looked like a much older version of me – but utter shit.

There had to be something better than being used as a sex toy and then drying myself in a concrete toilet block with green paper towels – there had to be more than this in my life.

The one good thing was that I wasn't tied down with possessions. My fleece was still in Jess' tent but my phone and wallet were in my pockets and that about summed up my life: a life in two pockets of smelly jeans.

I walked back to the tent and James was doing a fry up. I didn't know how he had the energy after last night.

21

He was friendly and offered me egg and bacon but I didn't fancy being with them. Having a drink and a laugh in the pub had been one thing but now, smelling like Manchester pavements an hour after the pubs have chucked out, it didn't feel right.

I had been useful last night – but that was it. I wasn't their friend and we all knew it.

I was right too. Jess appeared from her tent and I was pleased to see she looked as bad as me.

She held out my fleece. "I think this is yours…"

As if it could be anyone else's!

It was all I could do to mutter, "Thanks."

And to be honest, I think that we were both well embarrassed. We knew what we had done, and it wasn't anything to be proud of, so the sooner it was in the past and forgotten about, the better it would be all round.

James was a decent bloke and offered to take me back to my car in his Fiesta but, as I said, I felt like an outsider so I told him I'd walk down and enjoy the views of the Camel.

The river did look beautiful down below which cheered me up no end. I was glad about that because when I got to the car park there was a £60 fine on the windscreen for overstaying.

I needed a change…

*****

I went back to the caravan site and saw Mrs Moyle to see if she would do a deal on a longer stay. With the kids back at school, she was open to offers but I was desperate to preserve what I had from Tao and my only other money was the £85 giro from the Job Seeker's Allowance. Clearly, I was looking hard for a job in Cornwall – well, at least I was looking for something, even if I didn't know quite what it was.

Mrs Moyle came up with a fix which suited both of us. I could stay in the caravan for £75 a week if I would give Mr Moyle a hand with keeping the site tidy.

So, I did a lot of the manual work, because Mr Moyle was getting on. This took the morning and then the rest of day was free.

After Jess I didn't want any company. I didn't know what I wanted so I headed south to Kerensa Point where my mum used to sit with me and watch the sun go down.

She always let me have an ice-cream from the little wooden shop on the cliff top and one year she bought a shell for me which you could hold up to your ear and hear the sea.

I used to love that shell, and I had it for ages, until my brother threw it out of our bedroom window in a temper and it broke into zillion pieces in the yard below.

I expected it all to be changed now, and there be arcades on the Point and plastic seagulls, but it was either Kerensa or the Seal Sanctuary so I set off.

It was surprising how much I remembered. I was only a kid when we had driven down the narrow Cornish lanes but every now and again, I saw something which triggered a memory. There were still ponies in the farm next to the road and a trailer in a lay-by selling Cornish Pasties. It couldn't have been the same people but the trailer did look identical, still painted black with red writing on the side advertising "The Finest Authentic Cornish Pasties."

I drove over the crest of the hill and pulled to the side of the road. There, stretching out like a vast grey green carpet spotted with tiny flecks of white, was the wide entry to the English Channel. I hadn't become a sailor but just the thought of leaving Plymouth and heading for anywhere in the world made me stop and think.

Perhaps that ocean vastness was telling me that England had nothing to offer me. I had £100,000 in my bank account and this was a fortune in some parts of the world. Get a cheap flight, or a maybe even a place on a cargo ship. A lad at Uni had been on one

23

to South America and had a great time - and he'd finished his dissertation in peace and quiet.

Set off from Southampton and go to South America and start all over again, just away from all this shit.

But I was here now so I drove towards the sea and hoped that the little shop was still selling Cornish ice-creams.

*****

The last couple of miles always used to be in a bad state but it was a proper mess now. The final bit, down to the Point, was really narrow when dad drove us down there but now it was almost blocked with bracken, gorse and dog rose mounting a proper invasion of the road.

There was a layby, where one road went off to the old house, and a car was parked there. It was a bit tight but I got my Mondeo tucked in behind. Then, I got my anorak out and headed towards the sea.

It was a shock when I reached the shop – or what was left of it. The shop had always been just a big wooden shed. It sat on a big block of concrete and this was still fine but now the windows had been broken, either deliberately or with the violent winter storms, so the inside was a real mess.

The wooden walls, once painted a lovely blue and white, were now grey and white with occasional shards of colour desperately clinging on to their former, glorious past.

It was so sad.

I gently stroked the rough surface and tried to feel how they had once been twenty years ago.

I was a million miles away, inside my memories, and this is why I didn't see the woman even when she first spoke to me.

"What're you doing here? This is private property. You need to go."

Her voice wasn't shouty, or anything, but it was bordering on the aggressive.

24

Describing her was difficult.

If Penny, the Artificial Intelligence woman, was perfect in every way the person speaking to me wasn't. She was about medium height with very light brown hair, streaked with blonde. It was blowing about all over the place in the stiff breeze.

She wasn't wearing any make-up and looked, well, ordinary.

What did stand out was that, although she wasn't very old, there were dark black lines under her eyes. Either she'd been out on the lash for the last week and needed some serious sleep, or she had a lot on her mind.

I smiled at her in the hope of getting a bit softer response in return.

"Look, I'm really sorry if it's private now but I used to come here as a kid and watch the sun set with my mum.

"And I got an ice-cream too, if I'd been good…"

"Yes, well it's closed now and it's private and you're not allowed here so you've got to go."

"Okay, I'm going but you should put a sign up or something so that people don't wander down here.

"Do you own it now, I mean the shop and everything?"

"It's none of your business who owns it.

"So go. Just go!"

And I should have done just what she said, except that with what had happened the night before I was very tuned into sadness and what a waste of time life can be. I saw two tiny tears forming inside the corners of her eyes and then starting to slowly escape down her nose to the shadows below.

"Look, I know it's none of my business or anything, so please don't get mad with me but you look sad."

"It is none of your business so clear off – just bloody go!"

And then more tears battled their way out of her eyes and she wiped her face with her anorak sleeve.

Why I waited I don't know.

Not even if you gave me £10 million could I tell you why I ignored all the common sense warnings of harassing a lonely female on an isolated bit of Cornwall and how she could pick up her phone and tell the police that I'd made dirty comments to her or, worse still, touched her or any of the other thousands of ways to ruin my life.

And they could have all so easily happened.

I should have gone straight away – immediately – and started praying that she didn't destroy me with one phone call.

But I didn't.

"You do look fed up. I'm having a crap time too which is why I've come down here to try to remember some of the good things from when I was a kid.

"My mum bought me a shell and she told me that if I put it up to my ear, even when we were back at home in Bolton, I would hear the sea.

"I did – and it always reminded me of Cornwall and the sea."

It would be wrong to say that she smiled but her face sort of softened a little bit – only a bit but enough to let me know that she had understood how important what I had said was to me.

Maybe it was me telling her something personal which made the next thing happen.

"I had a shell too and I used to listen for the sea in it. Grandad used to give me one every summer and he painted the outside with wavy blue lines, like the shop used to be."

I smiled. "That was just like mine. How weird that we both had the same shells – and with the same blue lines.

"Did your grandad get your shell from here?"

This time there was a proper sniffle, and two or three big tears rolled down her nose.

"What's up?

"Don't cry.

"I do want to know."

26

"It was my grandad's shop and he died and he left the shop to me and my sister.

"She doesn't want it and I can't afford to buy her half so it's just getting wrecked.

"So now you know. That's why I'm crying.

"Just go away and leave me alone!"

No man with two bits of brain to rub together would have stayed a second longer. I'd made a woman cry and she'd told me to leave her alone. At this point I could already see the inside of the police cell.

But I did stay.

"If I sit on the rocks, a long way from you, will you tell me what happened?

"And then I promise that I'll go straightaway. I will honestly. I just don't like seeing you upset.

"Like I said, I've been having a crap time too so I do know a bit about how you feel and if you tell me your story I'll tell you mine and then perhaps we can both feel a bit less fed up."

She sat up and faced me – almost eye to eye. "I don't know why I am doing this, but okay. But if you start anything though, or start laughing at me or anything you've got to go."

I just nodded and said, "Sure."

"My grandad was a lobster fisherman. One day he was heading back with his pots and a storm blew up – like they do in seconds here.

"He saw two young lads trying to make it back to the bay at the bottom of the cliffs. They'd been fishing for mackerel and got caught out.

"A wave tossed the boat over and Grandad rescued them both.

"Even though the conditions were terrible he got them both in his boat and back to shore but all three of them nearly died.

"One of the kids was Sir Kenver's son. Sir Kenver owned all the land round here.

"After what had happened, Grandad had done with the sea. He told me that that lobster fishing wasn't nearly as good as it looks on a summer's day – like when your hands are frozen in winter or you can't fish for a week because of storms.

"So he asked Sir Kenver if he could have space for a little shop and he was given the whole of the Point for free.

"Then, three years ago, he died. I desperately wanted the shop to sell my paintings but my sister hates me.

"She's a commercial lawyer in London and earns a fortune but she wouldn't help me. Business is business she says.

"She thinks I'm the loser in the family and that I deserve what I get – which is nothing.

"So here it is – abandoned and falling apart.

"No-one will lend me a penny for a wooden shed and she won't move on the price.

"I've worked and saved and done jobs I hated but I've still only got a hundred thousand and when it was valued three years ago, it was valued at £400,000 so her half of that is £200,000 – or I can go and jump off the cliff.

"£400,000 for a knackered shed which is falling down? That's mad – absolutely crazy!"

This time the girl did smile ever so slightly.

"You don't know anything about prices in Cornwall, do you?

"A little beach hut can sell for ¼ million so £400,000 for somewhere like this is a bargain."

"Do you want to know the rest of the story?"

I nodded.

"In Grandad's will it said that if neither of us wanted what he called his shop after three years, it would have to be put up for auction and whatever money it made divided amongst the whole family.

"The three years comes in three weeks from now so I've come down here to say goodbye to my dream."

There was a pause which went on for ages – and I don't mean like in films but for a properly long time.

Then I said two things.

One, you could expect from someone who was a decent human being and the other had to come from a person who didn't know what day it was.

"That's terrible. It's bloody awful! And your sister as well. I just don't understand it."

She sniffed again and wiped more tears, and a drivel of snot too, on the sleeve of her anorak.

And now for the bit which should never, not in a zillion years, have happened.

"I've been made redundant and they wanted to silence me so I've got £100,000 too. Do you think that your sister would sell it to us both? You could have one half for your paintings and I could have the other half for sea shells and things…"

My voice trailed off because I didn't know anything about shops or selling or seashells – or sod all except environmental grants. And a computer program was better than me at these now.

This was absolutely mad.

The woman backed away.

"Get stuffed you bastard! You total bastard laughing at me! How could you?

"You total loser!

"I should never have told you anything.

"If you come near me, you'll regret it."

And she tensed and picked up a large pebble.

"Go on! Just try it! Come near me and I'll kill you!"

Then she started to cry – long, sobs filled with sadness and the futility of the situation.

I backed a little bit further away along the concrete block and sat in silence.

Eventually I had to say something, "Your anorak sleeve is getting all wet.

"Want a hankey?

"It's nearly clean…"

She sniffed again and then took it from it me, wiped her eyes, and gave it back to me.

"Thanks."

There was another long silence.

"You know, I am serious. We can have half each, with a wall or a divider down the middle and you could do your paintings and I can sell shells.

Even to me, it sounded like a totally mad idea.

She looked at me with her hard, grey eyes. "So where'd you get £100,000 redundancy money? That's the sort of money my sister earns – not someone like you.

"Do you deal in drugs or something?"

So I told her and she laughed when I said that Penny could jump from one Artificial Intelligence office to another without having to get in her car or wait all day for a train which had been cancelled.

And when she laughed, her whole face changed and she looked lovely. Obviously, I didn't say that but I did smile at her and she didn't look away.

At the end I said, "Look, if you want proof of how genuine I am, I've just risked all my money – my whole life to be honest – in telling you all this because I've signed a monster non-disclosure agreement.

"Now I've told you and if you told anyone else I'd be dead.

"Does that make you feel any better?

Neither of us spoke.

"And I don't even know your name."

She sort of smiled again and said, "I'm Grace."

"And I'm Martyn. That's Martyn with a y not an i because my mum hoped that I'd be posh when I grew up.

"I failed!"

And once more a smile flickered, very briefly, across her face and again, she did look lovely.

"Okay, but if you let me down I really will kill you. I don't know how I'll do it but I'll kill you, because I loved my grandad and I want to open his shop again because that's what he'd want to happen."

Surprisingly, she hadn't let go of her big rock and now her knuckles went white, as her hand tightened on it.

"And you're not getting anything else either. It's just like a house share so you keep to your half and I'll keep to mine and that's it. Nothing else.

"I'll make an appointment at Lavisters, the solicitors in Truro. If you give me your phone number I'll text you and then I'll see you there.

I gave her my phone number and she just said, "See you then."

She got up - and then stopped. It was if what was about to happen was too much for her.

"Martyn, I am terrible with men. I've never even had a proper boyfriend, things are that bad.

"I just don't know what to do or say.

"But you sound different and you look at me, not like that, but you look as if you care – as if you want things to go right for me. I've never had a man look at me like that.

"Martyn, please don't hurt me, if you can help it.

"When I've gone, don't laugh at me or text your mates saying that you met this soft cow who thought that you'd give her your money.

"Tell me you won't do that Martyn, please don't laugh at me behind my back."

Then more tears came. This was tearing her apart.

"You're not telling me lies, are you Martyn?"

I said very softly, "No. I'm not Grace. I don't know why we're

31

here together but there must be a reason so no, I won't laugh at you and I will do my very best for you.

I stood up and wanted to hug her – to reassure her that I would do my best and be with her. My hands sort of raised a little bit from my sides.

I wanted to let her know that I was here, and I would be, but it was too much risk. There were so many things which could go wrong.

She stood up and came ever so slightly towards me and her hands rose. There were two of us thinking the same thing.

It wasn't a real hug, and I never even kissed her cheek, but I needed to let her know I was there, on her side and that I would try to do my best for her.

"It might go wrong but I swear that I'll try my hardest – I swear that."

And I did.

CHAPTER THREE

CORNWALL, WE HAVE LIFT OFF (SORT OF)

Grace did text me. Somehow she'd got an appointment at the solicitors the following day.

I tried to sleep but couldn't so I got up in the middle of the night and wandered round the caravan site like a ghost looking for someone to haunt. I was out of my head with worry. I knew absolutely nothing about this woman except that she was definitely mad and probably violent – but she looked lovely when she smiled.

She could have five kids and a husband, or be on bail waiting to go to court for belting some bloke she didn't like, or anything else. There was not one grain of sense in going through with this.

I was still thinking that I couldn't possibly be doing what I was when I pulled into the long stay car park in Truro and got my phone out to look at Google Maps and find Lavister and Partners, Solicitors.

Spending £100,000 is surprisingly easily – if you've got a solicitor to help you.

The job took a couple of hours, with my bank needing lots of reassurance that I'd not done something insanely stupid like buying half of a knackered wooden shed, but Mr Lavister, who was the senior partner and was handling the whole probate, smoothed the way. I think he just wanted this whole thing closed and finished so that he could get back to some decently profitable work.

We both signed a contract to buy a derelict wooden shed piled up on a concrete block, sitting on a rocky cliff sticking out into the English Channel and that was that.

*****

We stood on the pavement with the old Victorian house where the solicitors were based at our backs. I glanced at the secretaries bustling around in the two ground floor offices. They had come to work this morning after taking their kids to school and getting stuck in the traffic and arriving late, with thoughts of what was going to happen if their husbands had to work in Qatar for three months and what they should do now they'd found out that their fifteen year old daughters were having sex.

These were the thoughts and worries which were on their minds – not two strangers who barely knew each other buying a pile of wood.

"Grace, do you fancy a cup of celebratory coffee – if we can afford it."

Then she did smile, a soft, warm, gentle, kind smile which said, "You've done the right thing Martyn, and I'm with you as much as you're alongside me."

*****

We found a little coffee shop away from the town centre. I bought us two old fashioned coffees and two old fashioned cakes, and we talked.

After a bit, the lady gave us a hard look so Grace bought us another two coffees and we talked some more.

I told her about Sarah and how she was going to be the one and only love of my life forever - and then how I found out that she wasn't.

Grace listened in silence and then, in the end, I had to ask her. "Well, is there anyone waiting for you back in Birmingham?"

She looked uncomfortable and then said, in a very flat voice. "No, there's no-one waiting for me. I've got friends but not, like that sort of friends.

"The truth is that I don't even have any proper friends any

34

more. I've been working at two or three jobs at the same time for three years and now I've lost touch with everyone.

"I wanted the shop more than anything else and there was nothing I wouldn't give up for it.

"During the day I worked in a call centre…"

And she pulled a face.

"Good morning madam. How can I help today? Oh I see. Your £1,000 dishwasher doesn't make your plates sparkle as you think it should. How incredibly interesting.

"How about you wash them yourself, you lazy cow?

"Then I worked nights waiting on in a posh gastro pub. Two of the chefs were off ill with 'flu one time and they were desperate so they asked if I could cook – you know, basic stuff like putting frozen chips in the fryer.

"I'd always cooked so this was easy and they let me do some of the other meals.

"It wasn't hard. Most restaurants serve ping food now. Stick it in the microwave, and three minutes later. Ping! And you're done. A scoop of chips, half a tomato and that's £25.

"They'd have let me stay on as a full-time cook, if I'd wanted.

"But there was better money cleaning the portable toilets which come back from shows and festivals.

"It's a filthy job cleaning cubicles and I used to stink rotten after a shift.

"So, call centre, pub, cleaning shit and then home at two o'clock in the morning ready for the next day.

"If you do nothing but work, and get free food from a pub, you can save up a lot of money."

I thought of how easy my life had been and didn't say anything for a long time.

Then I said, "You really did want the shop, didn't you?"

She was silent and just sipped her coffee.

The atmosphere was getting uncomfortable and of course, the

gremlins started screaming in my ears that I made the biggest mistake of my life by putting all my money into a mad scheme with a genuinely mad woman who would murder me if I said the wrong thing.

In the end I said, "Look Grace, we really need to think about the practicalities of how we're going to do this because although I've not been a toilet cleaner I'm sinking in the smelly stuff – and quick too.

"I've got no money except for the Job Seeker's Allowance and my credit card is running up like mad.

"And I know bugger all about running a shop.

"I've bet everything on this – and you."

A flicker of a smile crossed her face, "Okay, what do you want to do?"

Now that was a question because I didn't have bloody clue – not the vaguest idea!

Of course, what should have happened is that I ripped off my shirt and showed my Super Hero costume. Then I would have flown off in an amazing shower of sparks, re-built the shop in ten minutes and then zoomed back again.

That's what should have happened.

Instead, I said, "I suppose we ought to go and look at what we've bought" – in a totally unconvincing and very non-Super Hero voice.

*****

I did try, I really did, but Grace's mood had changed again and now she was not going to meet me half way – or even 1%.

I smiled, "Well since we're both going to the same place, do you want to come in my car or, if you'd rather, you can drive and then drop me off back here.

"I'm parked in the long stay."

No joy. She'd withdrawn again and the gremlins had come out for another pep talk in my right ear.

"Thanks but it's okay. It'll be better if we go in separate cars and then we're not holding each other up afterwards."

I tried hard not to tell her what I was thinking so I said, in the least non-confrontational voice I could manage, "Okay, I'm going back to my caravan and I'll see you down there tomorrow morning.

"Will ten suit?"

She got up, "Yes, that'll be fine."

Then she left. Just walked out – and that was that!

I was getting used to women using me and then losing interest straight after I'd done my duty.

*****

It was very busy going south the following day with a load of tourist traffic – I was already beginning to sound like a local – but I did have time to think.

I wished I hadn't.

Of course, I had a master plan and it was all worked out how I was going to work with a woman who'd kill me if I said a wrong word and how I was going to pay for my half of a new shop, then clean everything up and buy a load of sea shells to sell at a fortune.

It was easy.

The slight problem is that I didn't have a clue – not one bloody molecule of an idea what to do next.

My credit card debt was growing fatter by the day and eighty quid a week wasn't going very far, not at all.

I drove down the little lane towards the shop, our shop now, past the huge 19th century house, high on the hill, which sat like a big guard dog looking down on our little promontory.

I still didn't have an idea of what I was going to do when I saw the chain across the little, overgrown track leading down to the shop. It was a no messing about chain – a proper, heavy duty industrial, keepy-outy sort of chain and hanging from it was a printed sign stuck on a piece of wood.

It said, "No entry. Keep out. For all enquiries visit the Estate Office."

Well, that was a full hand of cards. Blow a hundred grand on going into business with a woman I don't know, doing something I don't know how to do and now I'm locked out. Bloody brilliant!

Oh look, an alien spaceship has just landed in the middle of that field of sheep and now I'm going to get blasted with a brain melting death ray.

No, that can't be right because I've already had my brain blown to pieces when I signed the contract in Truro.

As I was sat there, wondering was next on the crap delivery service, I heard Grace's car pull up behind me.

She got out and looked at the sign. Then she said, "What's happening? They can't have closed it off. How do we get to the shop?"

I was past caring now. "How the bloody hell should I know? You're the sodding expert. It was your grandad – not mine.

"Christ, what the bloody hell have you got us into?"

She was silent.

"Look, get in my car and let's see if we sort out this balls up."

She did get in and sat there in silence while I drove us up to Lowen Hall.

The Estate Office was off to the left, at the side of the Hall, and the stoned car park was almost empty.

We went in and there was an older lady sat behind an untidy desk.

I said, "I'm Martyn Hassall and this is Grace Felton my partner – my business partner. We own the shop on the Point and there's a chain across the road down to it."

She smiled, "Oh yes, Mr Cunnack's shop. How sad that he died. He was such a lovely person. We do miss him so…

"I think that Mr Adams wants to speak to you.

"I'll just phone him. I'm sure that he'll be down to see you in a couple of minutes.

"Would you like a coffee, or a tea, while you're waiting?"

I wanted to say, "No I don't. You can stick your tea right up where the sun don't shine.

"And I want your bloody chain removing - and now!"

But instead, I just said, "No thanks." And I wondered whether Grace thought that I was a soft limp wrist or just good at keeping my temper under control.

We didn't have to wait long.

The bloke who came to see us looked like a cartoon character of a farm manager – in his 40s, wearing a checked flat cap, jacket with leather elbow patches, those sort of velvety rural trousers and battered, but still polished, brown leather shoes.

He held out his hand and I was conscious that he was being very careful not to crush me because it felt like I was being held by the grabber on the front of a digger.

He was even more careful with Grace and sort of held his thumb and forefinger round her hand and gently touched each side.

"I'm Ben Adams, Sir Tristan's Estate Manager. Thanks for coming to see us.

"I know the chain across the lane wasn't what you wanted to see but we needed to talk before you did anything else.

"You also need to know that the lane is our property and we say who goes down it."

He was completely calm but I got the same feeling that a cow must have when it's being chosen for tomorrow's dinner.

"Sir Tristan would like a word, if that's okay?"

Of course, it wasn't a question at all – not in the slightest degree.

"Tell me moo cow, how do you feel about being the main course on the menu?"

"Pru, could you please phone Sir Tristan and tell him that we'll be right up?"

Then he turned to us, "If you don't mind following me…"

We crossed a stone paved yard and went into the main house. It was spectacular - if you like those sort of Gothic horror movies.

There was beautifully polished wood everywhere and the sun streamed through magnificent stained glass windows. Yet it still had the feel that it was someone's house, with a rack by the side door for two pairs of green wellies, an ancient Barbour jacket and a well-worn umbrella.

In front of us was a huge staircase which split two ways at what must have been the first floor. I was well wound up but couldn't stop myself from thinking that there was more carpet on the first five steps than there had been in the whole of my flat. This really was a different world.

We crossed what I supposed you could call the entrance hall, although it was big enough to be an industrial unit, and the Adams bloke knocked at a door which was at the far end.

He waited until he heard a voice say, "Come on in. It's always draughty out there."

We went into what was another Gothic horror set, right down to a suit of armour in a corner.

There was an elderly man and he got up from behind his huge mahogany desk which was cluttered with paper, books, pens and even two toy diggers. I wondered what Melissa would have thought of the mess.

He smiled at us - a real, honest, genuine smile and said, "Thanks for coming. I'm Tristan Lowen.

"I'm glad that you seem to have survived meeting Mr Adams - the Estate's rottweiler.

"So, you have completed the purchase of Jago's shop.

"I'm so pleased."

I must have looked startled and he smiled again. "Oh, don't worry about confidentiality or any of that nonsense. Cornwall is truthfully only one very big village and those people who need to know things get to know them.

"Those who did know thought that I should be told.

"Come on. Please relax and let's have a chat."

He motioned to the ginormous couch, a bigger brother of the one we'd sat in at the solicitors, and then said, "Would you mind getting us some coffee Ben - and chocolate biscuits, the ones cook gets with the thick chocolate?"

He patted his stomach. "At my age, I've given up worrying about my waistline."

He had that lovely, melodic, Cornish accent and turned to Grace, "Now then fair maid, let's see what we can do to help you and Martyn."

In some ways, I think that Grace was in a bigger mess than me. All that I had to lose was my £100,000 and I didn't have that a few weeks ago so, in a funny sort of way, I wasn't going to miss it.

I'd soon find another job which needed someone who knew their way round computers and forms, whether this was in England or abroad. At least for now, I'd be fine.

For Grace, there was much more to lose. She had her life invested in the shop – all the awful jobs, the stress and going without everything. I hardly knew her but even so I'd never seen anyone like this. She looked utterly defeated, beaten into the ground. She sat with her hands on her knees and even her head was down.

She looked so sad that I wished she'd stand up and have a go at Sir Benbum or Lord Low Arse or whatever he was - tell him to get stuffed and open up his lane so that we could get to our shop.

Sir Tristan noticed her sadness too, and in that soft accent again, said, "Well fair maid, you don't look too happy."

Adams came back in with a tray of cups, a big plate of chocolate biscuits and a polished silver coffee pot, milk in a little porcelain jug and some brown sugar lumps in another silver bowl.

Sir Tristan turned to Grace again, and said, "What can I get for you?"

But she just shook her head. She was beaten – we were beaten – and we both knew it.

The rest of us helped ourselves and Sir Tristan put three biscuits on his side plate. He had a long pull at his milky coffee, a good half of a chocolate biscuit, and then he put his cup down and spoke.

*****

"Ben, can you please explain the situation to Mr Hassall and his business partner?"

Being a properly old fashioned countryman, Ben had an A4 notebook instead of an iPad.

He turned over the first page, "Well, the first problem we have is the access road.

"As I said, it belongs to the Estate and if you want us to maintain it then it's not going to be a cheap job – especially now because it's not had any work done on it for three years.

"But we want to be fair so let's say £5,000 to keep the hedges neat and tidy and the road clear of potholes."

I felt as if I'd just been hit in the stomach by some professional kick boxer.

He continued.

"We own the power line and the water supply. The best way forward is for us to put a meter on the pole where the line down to the Point starts.

"I spoke to our agent and he thinks that you will use around £3,500 of electricity a year – plus VAT of course.

"The water will be a lot cheaper – say £1,000.

"Then we'll need a service fee for the little toilet block you've got down there and there will be business rates too.

"I think that all in you will need £15,000.

"How does that sound?"

I'd heard of tinnitus but never experienced it until then. There was a deafening, rushing in my ears as if a hurricane was howling inside my head.

I just felt empty.

I said, "That's going to be hard for us."

Grace was silent.

Sir Tristan put his coffee down, "May I have a word now, please, Ben?"

He looked directly towards us, but more at Grace than me.

"Let me try to explain a bit about me and your grandfather."

Incredibly, Grace briefly touched my knee – and then immediately withdrew her hand. I knew that she needed some comfort, just old fashioned support, and I wanted to give it to her but I couldn't help – not here, not now.

"In 1971, I was 18 years old. I'd finished school and scraped two not very good "A" levels and I was, what you might say, a bit of a lad.

"There was a lot of drinking, a lot of time spent with the village girls and the warnings from the police were getting more serious.

"I was out with Davy, who was Benjamin's dad, fishing for mackerel in his little 18 footer.

"The seals were watching us and spiking – popping their heads out of the water begging for mackerel – and I was having a great time.

"Davy said the weather was turning, and fast, and that we should be getting in straightaway. But I said no, and it's difficult to argue with the son of the man who employs you.

"So we stayed out, the squall hit us and the boat capsized. It's easy to say because it happened that fast. Three or four minutes from having a laugh to drowning – that's all it took.

Then he turned directly to Grace. "Your grandfather saved us both that day. Davy was hanging on the side of the boat but I was drowning. And that's the absolute truth. I was going to die.

"When I got back to the house, my father sent me to get changed and then ordered me down to see him, here, in this office. I was sat just where you are today Grace, but on a black chair.

"He gave me an ultimatum – and no options. Either I joined the army, as he had done at my age, or I took a proper course in estate management or I was on my own. Choose one - and now!

"I loved my dad, and I liked him, but sometimes he was ruthless.

"So off I went to university in Southampton and found that I actually liked learning the nuts and bolts of running our estate.

"I did well too and worked hard here during the holidays so my father started to listen to me more and more.

"In January 1974, which was my final year, we were all taken to the London docklands to see what a mess the place was in. The docks were nearly all closed and the whole area was just a massive wasteland – like something from the war in Ukraine.

"The three day week had kicked off with non-stop strikes and power cuts and no-one had any hope that it would ever be any better.

"Without telling anyone, I came back the following weekend and walked along the river in the sleet and rain and started thinking that one day this mess would all be redeveloped: it had to be.

"So, I went back to my father and asked if we could start buying parcels of land.

"It was a real mess with the docks being owned by so many different companies – the Greater London Council, Local Authorities, British Gas – everyone had a say.

"But my father was very clever at seeing a way through.

"I used to smile when I watched him in action.

'Would you like to discuss selling a small parcel of land Mr Politician? And do bring your lovely lady wife with you when we have dinner at my villa in the British Virgin Islands and talk about the future.'

'And yes Mr Surveyor, we will have a consultancy post ready and waiting for you when you decide to retire.'

"All very honest and above board - but the way to get things done.

"In 1981, the whole 8 square miles – that's the size of a small city – was developed by Environment Minister Michael Heseltine and we made a lot of money – an awful lot of money – in the next ten years.

"Now, my three children have vastly more money than they need, or deserve – as I do too."

Then he paused and looked at Grace.

"How can I help you and show my gratitude to your grandad?"

*****

He looked past us and said, with a huge grin, "Well then Ben, what do you think that we could do to get this lovely team in action?"

I didn't know what to think. "You're going to help us then?"

Ben was laughing too. "Well me 'ansome, we'll certainly have a try."

"Do you want me to let them know your thoughts, Sir, or would you rather do it?"

"No, no, no. You're the expert Ben and you've done all the hard work. I've just been a spectator."

Then Sir Tristan turned to Grace, "You'll like this fair maid."

Ben began. "We did our homework on the costs because we thought that you would never be able to buy the shop.

"Sir Tristan had more confidence in you than I did but if it came up for auction, we would have bought it and cleared the site. So, we know a fair bit of what needs doing.

"And we also know a little bit about your position because," and he smiled at Grace, "every time you visit the village shops there are ears listening.

"The road down to the shop can't be used as it is. We'll start clearing it tomorrow.

"Sir Tristan has already approved four or five loads of tarmac to be laid and then it will be fine.

"But before we can do this, we've got another idea. The shop is just firewood so we'll bring this up to the small paddock behind the hall and have a bonfire."

He must have seen Grace's look of horror.

"Don't worry Miss Grace, we've got another idea.

"When we were having a lot of contractors on site we had a big meeting room, like those mobile homes you see, so that we didn't have strangers traipsing in and out of the Estate Office.

"It's sat there empty now, if you'd like it – sort of a very early Christmas present. And it's free.

"We can just squeeze it down the lane and the boys will have it on the concrete base in a flash.

"It's got two parts plus a toilet and a little kitchen.

"Perfect for a shop."

And Sir Tristan actually cheered and clapped when Grace said, "Thank you so much Sir Tristan. I don't know what to say."

"Then best you don't say anything because Ben has some more good news."

"When your new shop is settled, we'll have a go at the electric and water supply and I can't see any need for meters, or any of that rubbish, can you Sir?"

And he nodded his head to Sir Tristan.

"No, no – life is too complicated as it is without meters and checking and all that nonsense.

"But carry on Ben…"

"Well, we know that you two are staying in different accommodation and neither your caravan" and he turned to me, and then

Grace, "nor Mrs Bennett's bed and breakfast is convenient for the shop so we have something for you to consider.

"During the renovation, specialist contractors sometimes needed to stay on site, if they'd been working very late.

So we let them stay in one of the Estate's holiday lodges.

"It's a bit knocked about, because contractors aren't exactly respectful of where they are staying, but we'll get it cleaned up and very liveable.

"We know that you two aren't together, as it's said these days, but you'd each have your own private space until the shop is making a fortune and you can afford your own places.

"Sir Tristan has given permission for Mrs Haldicott to put your washing in with the house's laundry so you can concentrate entirely on the shop.

"Well, what do you think?"

The last month had taught me one big lesson. You never know what's coming next – and I didn't this time.

Grace almost leaped round Sir Tristan's desk and gave him a long, long hug and an equally long kiss on his cheek.

"I don't know what to say. I'm so grateful. I don't know what to say."

"Well fair maid, best you don't say anything then…"

I can't remember what Grace, or Ben, or Sir Tristan or even I said next. There were some bits of useful information but mainly a lot of smiles and kind reassurance.

At last, I thought that we were going to do this – we actually were.

Ben escorted us through the house and back to the Estate Office, thanked us for coming and then said he would see us tomorrow.

We walked to our cars and then came the inevitable tension. I wondered if I was about to run into iceberg Grace again.

I spoke first. "Well, I'll see you tomorrow, then."

Grace looked at me with her grey blue eyes but now they were softer than I had ever seen them before.

47

"Thanks Martyn. Thank you so much. I never had anyone who'd stand with me – who'd be alongside me and, well, you know.

"I know that I can be hard work but I've had a terrible time and now, at last, things are going to get better – I just know they are.

"You will sell millions of sea shells and ornaments and things and I can show people my paintings. We're going to make a go of this, I'm sure that we are."

And like I've said, you never know what's coming next but I was so glad that when Grace gave me a long hug I felt the softness of her cheek against mine and thoughts began which were a bit more than flogging sea shells.

*****

If the hug was a shock what came next was from another planet.

Grace giggled, "I'm really looking forward to flat sharing with you…" and she giggled again. She did. "Well, lodge sharing which is nearly the same.

"I can go back to Mrs Bennett's tonight and give her a week's notice. She's been very kind to me so that's only fair.

"But what about you?"

I was actually embarrassed. "It's about the same for me except that the caravan is only bloke tidy and clean and I can't give it back like that."

And in this crazy mad world where I lived now, Grace said, "Well, I'll follow you back to your place and help you get it nice.

"If that'd be a help?"

"No, it wouldn't be just a help – it'd be a bloody miracle!

"I keep things clean and a bit tidy but I'm no good at the stuff which seems natural to women – and I don't care if that sounds sexist and old fashioned because it's true."

*****

48

I opened the door to the caravan and Grace stepped inside. Then she gave me that special look reserved for blokes who don't know anything about making a house properly presentable.

Grace was a genius. There was an old fashioned vacuum cleaner in the caravan and she used this like some super weapon. What would have taken me hours, she did in about ten seconds.

The results were miraculous – and I said so.

Then Grace said, "Right then. Since we're business partners…" and she smiled "let's have a business meal."

I was right up for this and I said, "Well, the microwave is pretty good so I can go into the village and get a pizza or, if you want to celebrate, I'll treat us to fish and chips.".

Grace actually did put her hands on her hips. "Do you eat like this every night? It's no wonder you're short of money.

"What proper food have you got?"

Before I could answer, she had flung open the door on the little fridge. I don't know what she expected to find but I bet it was a bit more than half a "Value" sandwich from a meal deal.

"Martyn, haven't you got anything? Is there anything at all I can use?"

I looked genuinely embarrassed – because I was.

"Okay. Don't touch a thing – not one bloody thing!

"Just look at your phone or text somebody but keep everything tidy or you'll be doing it all yourself.

"I'm going into the village to see what I can find."

She didn't have a rock in her hand this time but her voice was just as threatening so I found a YouTube video of last year's Italian GP at Monza, sat up straight so I didn't disturb the cushions Grace had fluffed up, and watched some epic racing.

I didn't have long to wait before Grace bounced in with a 30p Bag-for-Life containing what might be our tea.

Grace never even asked me where the pans were but found them herself.

She laid everything out next to the cooker. If the idea was to impress me, it certainly worked. There were two chicken breasts, red and yellow peppers, a little bottle of olive oil and a combined salt and pepper thing, some herb stuff in a small glass jar and, last of all, a packet of fusilli.

I knew it was fusilli because the one-and-only-love-of-my-life-forever used to cook this for us – when she wasn't screwing behind my back.

She said that it tasted better than other pasta stuff and I agreed. I was just grateful that she cooked, because I couldn't.

Grace actually smiled when she said, "I don't know why I'm asking this but you've not seen a big knife and a wooden spoon or anything like, have you?"

Well, actually I had. I knew that there was a big knife and I knew where it was too – so take that Ms Supercookerwoman! It wasn't there to defend myself against Jess using me as a sex toy again but I'd had it to free the stuck blind on the big window next to my bed.

I thought that I would score some Brownie points when I retrieved the knife and presented it to Grace but she looked at me like I was a cat who'd just given her a dead mouse.

"Bloody hell! What've you done to it? It's a crap knife but you still can't use it as a screwdriver. Haven't you ever cooked anything?"

I smiled and shrugged my shoulders and the amazing, and very, very wonderful thing was that she smiled too. When she wasn't threatening to kill me, she was nice.

Grace had found a wooden spoon in one of the drawers and started cooking. It was amazing how fast she was: chop, chop, chop, cut, cut, cut: chuck it all in the pan and it was on our plates in minutes.

Bloody hell! It was good too. I told her so and she smiled. "I sort of learnt from my mum but I could always cook. That pub where I worked offered me a proper job but the pay's crap cooking every day unless you work in a top restaurant - and it's brutal hard work.

"I made more money at the Call Centre – and I wasn't bent over a stove for hours on end either.

"But thanks for the compliment. It's been nice to cook for someone else, instead of just me."

While she'd been cooking, I'd made us two cups of coffee and she held one up to me now.

"Cheers. We'll have champagne soon…"

But I knew that there was going to be a lot to do before we'd even be able to afford a bottle of cheap Australian plonk.

CHAPTER FOUR

WHERE TO NOW?

I did offer to sleep on the sofa bed at the front of the caravan so that she could have my bed but when I mentioned this, the temperature dropped again and Grace said that she needed to go back to her B&B. It was like she said - as if she'd come from a different planet and didn't know anything about blokes, even the most basic stuff – the things you learn as a young teenager.

So, the next time that I saw her was at the Point. She'd got there before either me or Sir Tristan's men, dressed like she always was in baggy pants and top, and looking like she was ready for the next challenge on Celebrity SAS.

Whatever else you could say about Grace, and I did have a lot of different thoughts, I have never seen anyone work so hard or with such enthusiasm. Her only concession to safety, if you can call it that, was a pair of leather gardening gloves and she needed these as she tore into the derelict shop and loaded the wood on to the trailer.

The way that she worked did have a big effect on everyone else. Sir Tristan's blokes saw her getting stuck in, and with a smile, so they joined in with her and the remains of the dead shed were on the way to the bonfire by lunch-time.

Grace had got a little camping gas stove from somewhere and so in between humping wood she made tea for everyone and, in a funny sort of way, led the team. It wasn't that she was pushy, or the official boss or anything like that, but more that everyone could see how much she wanted to succeed.

Because she believed in what she was doing, so did everyone else – including me.

As Sir Tristan had said, Cornwall is just a big village and the word soon got back to the house about Grace. At lunch-time, the lads went up to their crew room on the estate but not before one of them had brought us a big plate of sandwiches - beef and pickle, and some Hevva cakes that had been made in the house.

Grace made us some more tea and we sat together on the concrete block looking out over the grey green sea.

When she wasn't looking, I had a sly glance at her and I was beginning to believe that we were going to make a success out of this crazy scheme. Of course, she was as mad as a box of frogs who'd been smoking dope but I'd never met anyone who believed, really believed, in anything before – not because they were being paid to believe, or they were in group who all cheered at the same things at the same time, but because there was a fire inside her which nothing could put out.

The lodge still needed what Ben called, "A bit of tidying…" so I went back to my caravan and Grace to her place.

I smiled when she warned me to keep the caravan immaculate because, one way or the other, it had to be returned tomorrow and she wanted it to be pristine.

As I drove north, I couldn't stop thinking about being warned to keep the caravan perfect when it wasn't even hers and we were only business partners – not even friends.

The worrying thing is that I wanted her to care – with her flashing eyes and white knuckles as she picked up the rock to bash my head in. What was worse was that I was missing being with her.

*****

I put the alarm on early for the following day. I wanted to see Mrs Moyle and thank her for letting me stay in the caravan. She came in and made lots of cooing noises about how nice I had kept it and if I ever wanted a full-time job there would be one there waiting for me. AIs were brilliant at filling in forms but you'd never get Penny with a strimmer.

It was half past ten before I got to the Point and Grace knew where I'd been but, even so, there wasn't much of a welcome.

She'd really got this whole job by the throat and she and Ben were walking up and down the entry lane looking at the width.

Grace was worried about our shop – our free shop given to us for nothing by Sir Tristan, remember – getting down the road without being scratched.

She had the cheek to be arguing the odds with Ben and the lads. The issue was a rock which was stuck out from the bank and Grace was sure it would damage the unit.

Ben was certain that everything would be fine, although it would be a tight squeeze, so of course the boys did what Grace said and got stuck in with a pickaxe and a crow bar and the rock was removed.

The lads thought it was hilarious that Ben had been told what to do by Grace.

It took a brilliant bit of driving to get the trailer down the lane with the unit hanging off each side but late in the afternoon it was there.

It was nearly finishing time for Sir Tristan's men but Grace wanted the unit on the concrete block immediately – so they stayed and wriggled it off the trailer on to the base just because Grace wanted it there so badly.

You know how everything is these days, with an excuse for whatever happens but Grace was different. She believed in whatever we were doing and so did everyone else. It wasn't any more complicated than that.

*****

The next big chasm, for me at least, was moving in with Grace. It was only like a flat share but it was a long time since there'd been a woman in my private space.

54

She got to the lodge before me. It was only April so it was still a bit chilly. Grace had put on the Calor gas heating and it was nice to come in to somewhere warm.

Like me, she was travelling light and all her stuff was packed into her little Fiat.

I was actually a bit nervous when I opened the door but she smiled and said, "You look shattered. Would you like a cup of tea?"

"That'd be lovely. Working with you is a bit full on.

"Look, I'm easily pleased so which bedroom would you like?"

Grace shrugged her shoulders.

In actual fact, both bedrooms were almost identical but one faced where the sea was, even if it couldn't be seen, and so I chose this.

Grace was friendly but only in a flatmate sort of way.

"Look, we both know that you can't even put a tin of beans on a slice of toast so I don't mind cooking. I'm fast and we'll save a lot of money this way.

"If you do the washing up, and keep everything tidy, then I'll be happy.

"I also need you to work out what we're doing next every day because I want everything to be ready for the May Day Bank Holiday and that gives us two and a half weeks.

"You did planning for a job," and this time she actually did smile "so plan this for us and leave the cooking to me."

Grace was brilliant, even in a little kitchen, and she was fast too. We had burgers, grilled tomatoes and chips and it took her about ten seconds. I could see why they wanted her to cook for a living.

Afterwards, Grace said that she had some catching up to do so she went to her bedroom, drew the thick room divider across: and that was that. I mean, that was that in every sense of the word!

I was actually glad that the dining room lounge was between us. I did all my bathroom stuff, closed my room divider and didn't

55

even look at my phone. I was on my last legs – physically and emotionally and I could have slept on one of the gorse bushes outside with a sheep eating my toes.

So to say that I was hard on, fast asleep, would be a lie. I was actually unconscious when Grace's alarm went off at half past five. Bloody hell! This time in the morning was only to get into Silverstone for F1 before the roads got jammed - and I couldn't see any Ferraris racing down our road!

By the time I had come round, well a bit anyway, the shower was running. I was still in bed when Grace shouted through my divider, "Shower's free. Come on. We've got a busy day."

And she was right.

I still wore a watch. I like watches. They're quiet and reliable. You know where you are with a watch. It doesn't give you opinions or record what you say for a TikTok film. It just tells you the time and that's it.

I looked at my watch when I got down to the Point – five minutes after Grace. My reliable watch said 6.15. That's quarter past six in the bloody morning! She must have been mad - and I was as bad because I was here with her.

She'd got a trowel and screwdriver from somewhere and was on her knees, in her baggy pants, attacking the weeds which had grown in every available crack.

When the lads came down two hours later, she'd got a pile of weeds out – and I was becoming better and better with the big yard brush she had found for me.

The problem for we ordinary humans was that we couldn't ignore her energy and enthusiasm or pretend it didn't exist – because it did, and tons of it. She wanted the shop to open and it was as if she had a nuclear bomb inside her. If you've ever heard of generals leading from the front, it was Grace.

This was amazing but as Sir Tristan's lads did their jobs with the electricity, water and toilets I was beginning to have other thoughts.

Attacking everything Kamikaze style was fine but I was good at planning and I knew that we needed more than that..

Although I had been replaced by a computer programme, I had made a lot of money for Tao Visions by being methodical and organised - and Grace was neither.

In the middle of the morning, she made everyone tea. I needed it but I was starving hungry too. There was no eating on the job with atomic Grace, and breakfast had been four hours ago.

The lads sat in their van which was good because it gave us a bit of space and privacy.

Maybe it was because I was starving hungry or perhaps I had run out of enthusiasm or, most likely, I was simply fed up with Grace's idea of a normal life.

Whatever the reason, I knew that we needed to talk.

I was quite formal because I was back in full work mode – my work.

"Look Grace, you've done a fantastic job getting the shop down here and Ben and the lads to sort out all the logistics," I soon defaulted to my old planning days, "but if we are ever going to make a go of this shop, we can't do it just by running round like mad things."

Grace was silent at first, then she asked, "Do you know what to do?

"For the last three years I've thought about nothing but getting the shop and then selling my paintings.

"I've never had a business and I don't know anything about all the business stuff. Do you?"

Of course, I wanted to tell her that I had run twenty-seven successful businesses and I was actually a multi-millionaire in disguise: but I couldn't.

"I'm not much better off than you because I've never had a business either but I do know all about stuff like business accounts, tax returns – and Health and Safety warnings on the step up to the shop."

Grace actually did look at the three steps and smiled.

"Why don't you go back to the lodge and make a start on…"

There was a long pause.

"Well, on sorting things out."

"Thanks but I want to stay down here and watch you beat up Sir Tristan's blokes.

"I think it's important for them to see that we're both getting stuck in – it's our shop after all."

And I was being honest. I did want them to see that we would get our hands dirty – but there were other reasons too.

I was enjoying feeling my body working. I did go to the gym, a bit anyway, and I cycled, but too much time at Tao was spent sat looking at a computer screen. Then there was F1 on the telly when I came home and Netflix and a bit of porn and a glass of wine, or two, until it was too late to do anything that day and so I made a promise to make the effort tomorrow – and rarely did.

This was different. It wasn't heaving weights up and down for nothing or cycling going nowhere. If my muscles ached it was for a reason and I liked making the effort.

I even looked at the little blisters on my hands with pride. They hurt but they'd got there by doing something real.

So this was all the caveman stuff. All that I needed now was a flint spear and I'd be bringing back a Woolly Mammoth over my shoulder for Grace to cook tonight.

But there was another reason. Right from the first moment I'd met Grace there'd been something about her. I mean, it wasn't just that I'd never had a woman threaten to belt me with a big rock before, or the way she treated me like a parking warden she'd just had an argument with.

She was different – honest and passionate, and I'd never met anyone like her.

There was something else too – and it was properly weird. I

liked being with her. We weren't even friends but I enjoyed her company and I just couldn't deny it.

*****

We were both quiet when we got back to the lodge.

Grace was covered with a layer of grey Cornish dust and said, "I need a shower before I can cook dinner.

"You go into your bedroom so that I can get changed."

There was no, "Would you mind awfully dear Martyn to protect my maidenly modesty..."

Just do it.

She was quick getting washed and when she called me through she was dressed in another one of her baggy uniforms. There wasn't a trace of make-up and her hair was a real mess but somehow she looked like she behaved: honest. She was what she was and you either accepted it or didn't – and I got the feeling that she wasn't bothered one way or the other.

There was a piece of paper on the dining room table. "Can you go into Helston and get these," and after a little pause added, "please?"

"There are proper supermarkets in Helston. It's not too far and you'll be sure of getting everything.

"I'll cook something for us while you're away."

And there was another pause.

"We're making fantastic progress and I don't think that I could do it without you.

"Thanks.

"I really do mean that.

"Do you like wine?"

Of course, I couldn't say, "Yes Grace I do – but not more than a couple of bottles at a sitting."

So I was sensible and said, "Yes, I like a glass of wine with a fabulous meal. I wonder where I'll get one tonight?"

And do you know, Grace actually laughed – a proper laugh and showed her teeth and the lines round her eyes and she did look lovely.

I went into Tesco in Helston with the list - and the problems started the moment I walked through the door.

In my previous existence, and that seemed like a million years ago, I was okay with frozen pizzas and ready meals and I knew all about the alcohol section, and where to get the quality Nacho chips.

Unfortunately, none of these man vital items was on the list so I found a nice Tesco lady, about my mum's age, and she took me round like some numpty who was on day release and together we got all the things Grace had ordered.

She even had a special, gentle, very calm Man-Thickie voice so I guess I wasn't the first lost soul who'd been sent shopping by their wife or girlfriend or nutty lodgemate.

I didn't need my Tesco mum to find the wine. I knew everything about buying booze and I got a bottle of Australian Shiraz. £10 was more than I would have spent on me but this wasn't for me – it was for us and I couldn't give Grace a bottle of cheap plonk: it wouldn't have been right.

I was grateful for what Grace was doing and I wanted to show my appreciation so I bought a big black and white bag with a surfer on it and "Love Cornwall" across both sides.

When I got back to the lodge, the smell hit me straightaway when I got out of my car. I couldn't tell you what all the individual stuff was but it said, "Eat me because I'm delicious."

And bloody hell, it was!

Grace had made a sort of pie, with potatoes on top and beef and onions and mushrooms inside. It was fantastic.

She said that Mrs Teague, Sir Tristan's cook, had given her the ingredients – and with a smile too. But that from now we were buying our own things – or going hungry.

After the beef pie, or whatever it was called, we had some doughnuts that I'd bought from Tesco.

Everything was lovely and I was absolutely knackered – on my last legs.

This was the strange thing about Grace. She was a full-on pyscho who'd kill you if she didn't get her own way and yet at the same time she was kind – and considerate.

She said, "You go and start the planning for tomorrow and I'll do the washing up."

Of course, I said that wasn't fair but she was having none of that nonsense so I went to my bedroom, got out the big A4 pad I'd bought in Tesco and started planning.

If my body had enjoyed the physical work, my mind had an even bigger smile when it was asked to do things it was good at.

To start, I turned the pad sideways and drew a flow chart. I just loved flow charts. I think that I must have been born drawing them.

We needed this and then this, followed by this and then this. It was lovely, and so relaxing. That's my excuse for not hearing Grace at first. Of course, having fallen asleep didn't help either.

"You can have the bathroom now. I'm finished."

And I heard her screen being firmly closed.

Five minutes later I was hard on, fast asleep.

CHAPTER FIVE

YOU NEVER KNOW YOUR LUCK IN LIFE'S RAFFLE

Over breakfast, I explained that the first thing we needed – actually more than the first – was some money.

I was still claiming Job Seekers' Allowance but this couldn't go on forever and in any case, £85 a week wasn't going to buy us very much.

At first, Grace was very defensive and said, "I'll pay for last night's stuff. I should have sorted it out with you straightaway."

This time I smiled. "Look, don't be a soft thing. How much do you think a meal like this would have cost me in a pub? I'd be lucky if I got away with thirty quid – and then there'd be a tip…

"Is there an automatic service charge here, madam?"

And a flicker of a smile very briefly crossed her face.

"All the stuff only cost £58, and that included the wine. I checked my credit card and I've still got £1500 wriggle room left on it. That's the truth. But I owe nearly two grand now and so I've got to be careful and we've got to earn some money.

"But fifty quid on groceries isn't the problem.

"We've got to buy some stock for me to sell and then insurance and all the rest of the health and safety crap.

"We can't run the business on fresh air and you beating people up.

"How are you fixed?"

Grace shrugged her shoulders. "About the same actually. I haven't had any paid work for six weeks now and I've been living on my credit card too.

"Wait on."

She poked her phone a bit and then said, "That's great. We should be sister and brother. I've got a £3,500 limit on my card and I've spent £2,000."

And she did laugh – but she didn't find anything funny in the situation.

"So no more wine for us and I hope that you enjoy cheap pasta because you're going to be eating a lot of it from now on."

There was another very long pause – I was getting used to these now with Grace.

"Look, let's forget dividing the shop. You've been brilliant. Even that's not right. You've been fantastic.

"So, we'll get the shop ready to open and I'll go to Birmingham, get my paintings and whatever we make we'll share.

"How does that sound?"

I couldn't say anything else but, "Thanks Grace – you're a star" and, except for the table between us, I would have given her a long hug.

*****

We were late getting down to the shop the following day. It had been a long three days and we were just too far gone for a dawn patrol.

The sun was really strong by the time we arrived and it was real, summertime hot. I stripped off my shirt and climbed up the step ladders to finish cleaning out the gutters.

Incredibly, Grace was still in her baggy uniform. I think that these were the only clothes she owned. She was beneath me, attacking the few remaining weeds, and I had my back to her. This is why I was shocked when I did turn round and saw that she had taken off her sack top and was just in a sort of a black sports bra thing.

I did look – and she went berserk.

"What are you staring at?

"Why are you looking at me like that?"

I didn't say anything. What do you say when you just turn round on a ladder and the next thing you're being accused of being a perv?

Grace was furious – absolutely ready to finish me off.

She screamed, "I know what's on your mind.

"You men are all the same. You're laughing at me because I've got no tits."

I nearly fell off the ladder.

"Grace, stop this – and don't be sounding like a slag – because you're not.

"I was just surprised to see you out of your baggy uniform – that's all Grace, nothing else."

I suppose it could sound as if I was asking to be forgiven but I wasn't. I just wanted everything to calm down.

But Grace was sobbing deep, hurt tears like I'd never seen before. She was inconsolable.

I climbed down the ladder and said, "Come on, I'll make us a cup of coffee and we'll eat the last of the chocolate biscuits because with what's left on our credit cards, we're going to be on a diet soon."

And I tried to smile.

I was stood next to her now and reached down to help her up.

I passed her the kitchen roll to wipe her tears and said, "Come on, tell me, what's the matter."

"Please don't laugh Martyn if I tell you – please don't otherwise I'll throw myself off the cliff, I will – I mean it, I will.

"I've never had boobs like all the other girls. They just didn't grow and all the other kids let me know. Even the teachers used to say things.

"Then I got to the age when everyone was letting lads touch them up and so I did as well.

"There was this one lad who was supposed to be cool and he squeezed me really hard because there was nothing there and when I cried he just got up and left me.

"The next day, he was going round everywhere saying Gracie had no tits and was more like an ironing board than a proper girl with real tits.

"And everyone knew that he was right. I've got nothing, and no bum either. I know what men want in a woman and it's not a bloody ironing board.

"That's why I never had a boyfriend.

"Then I started work and one of the managers wouldn't leave me alone. He was on to me all the time. At the Christmas party he told me that he loved me.

"He was married but said that his wife was leaving him and that he truly loved me.

"And of course I believed him.

"I was only 19, and I'd never been with a man and so it was all fantastic.

"He took me to his house one afternoon and said it was all going to be great.

"I wanted to go with him but when we got there I started to get worried.

"I'd never seen a man undressed before and I was frightened.

"Then he did it and he was so rough - and he hurt me.

"When I said how much he was hurting me he did get off me straightaway but I could see that everything had changed.

"The following day he hardly spoke to me and so I knew what had happened.

"I was so ashamed, and I was bleeding a lot, so I gave my notice and left that day.

"I walked past him at five o'clock and he never even looked up.

"I just thought that's how men are."

And she sobbed, achingly sad breaths from deep inside her.

What did I do? Well, nothing sensible and that's for sure.

Instead of keeping my distance, which was the only sane thing to do, I moved close to Grace and let her head rest in the nape of my neck. Then, I let her warm tears trickle down my naked chest and I stroked her hair very gently so that she knew I was there with her.

That's all that I did. Nothing else. Just one human helping another.

It didn't last long. Grace raised her head to look at me, "Thank you Martyn."

What could I say that wasn't going to be trite and hurtful or simply the wrong thing for some unimaginable reason?

So I didn't say anything at all but just smiled instead.

*****

There was still tons to do at the shop but we were both a bit subdued after what had happened. We were getting away with things for now but one day soon, something was going to go wrong and fate would bite us both right in the bum – and badly too.

Grace was on her hands and knees, scrubbing the floor until it shone and the new, all action DIY me was tightening the final screws in the long shelf on the back wall. Maybe this is why we didn't hear the Range Rover arrive.

It was Sir Tristan and Ben.

Grace saw who it was first and jumped up to greet them. I hoped that they didn't notice her red eyes from all the crying.

"Well then," said Sir Tristan, "you're developing quite a reputation in these parts."

And his face almost split in half with a grin.

"Anyone who can overrule our Ben must have balls of steel – and be a lot more of man than I am.

"So well done you.

"Everyone respects what you are doing and hard work means a lot in Cornwall. You're a proper louster, you are."

"She is that Sir Tristan and she's doing a bloody good job."

"Now where's that man of yours – hidin?"

"Not hiding Sir Tristan – just stood behind the boss, as I always am. I know my place."

And I smiled.

"And how are things getting on, me 'ansum – ready to start making some money?"

I know what I should have said. I needed to stand up straight and lie to Sir Tristan and tell him that everything was going brilliantly – but I couldn't. So, I told him the truth – well, mainly the truth.

"You've been brilliant Sir Tristan, and Ben has too, but we're going to have a few tough months.

"We'll get by because I can do some tidying and strimming in the evenings on the caravan sites, and I'm sure that Grace will get some shifts cooking in pubs - but it's going to be tough.

"We'll do it though."

Sir Tristan had pale blue eyes and a very calm face. He was always smiling and relaxed but you could see that underneath there was a serious brain at work.

"I'm sure you will but I wonder if you'd let us help a bit?

"Like I said before, I've got all the money that I'll never need and my kids have more than they should.

"When I see folks like you and Grace you touch a special place in me. You want this place to work and I want it too.

"I hope that you can see this.

"If I was 50 years younger, I'd be down here with you, weeding and painting - getting everything ready.

"There's part of me here because I walked over these same rocks, soaking wet and shivering, after nearly drowning.

"You doing well reminds me every day of how lucky I was," and he turned directly to Grace, "and what a wonderful man your grandad was.

"And that's it.

"Now, can I be allowed to help you a bit more?"

What to say? Since meeting Grace I was learning the importance of saying nothing so that's nearly, but not quite, what I did.

I reached out and shook Sir Tristan's hand, and then Ben's.

"Thanks so much. We're both so grateful for what you've done for us and we'd be glad for any help you can give us, anything at all."

Ben looked at Sir Tristan, "Can I Sir?"

"Yes, of course Ben, you did all the hard work."

Ben turned to me. "I'll phone you later and we'll work out a time for you both to come up the Estate Office and meet Mrs Kimbrell. She's responsible for the Estate's finances.

"She'll help you with all the boring stuff – I bloody hate it – accounts and insurance and all that.

"She'll also tell you about the bank account that she's set up for you.

"There's £35,000 in it now to get you going until you can pay your own way.

"You can look at it as an interest free loan – but there's no rush to pay it back, is there Sir?"

"No, no, just consider it a long term loan to get the boat launched and on its way.

"It's my pleasure to help you.

"See you dreckly then…"

Grace got in her hugging mode again – but not for me obviously – and I did some more handshaking and thanks.

Afterwards, I said to Grace. "That's too much for me. I said that some weird fate thing had thrown us together and it has.

"And we've hit the jackpot again.

"Grace we're going to do this, we are."

And, somewhat incredibly, I did get a Grace hug.

*****

I was working hard at the DIY stuff – and enjoying it – when Grace called, "Come on. Feeding time at the zoo."

She insisted that we couldn't carry on accepting sandwiches from Sir Tristan so she'd made cheese and tomato butties of our own.

As it happened, I knew about cheese and tomato sandwiches because I could make them. You got a slice of value cheese out of a packet and stuck it on a round of bread with a bit of tomato and that was that: a cheese and tomato sandwich.

Not Grace though. We had some nutty brown bread spread with real mayo and then thin slices of Cornish Cheddar and neatly sliced tomatoes, all seasoned with salt and pepper and each sandwich cut into two pieces.

Bloody hell! I could have lived forever on Grace's cheese and tomato sandwiches.

We ate our lunch and talked about this and that, nothing much really. We should have been having serious discussions about how lucky we had been but the sun was beating down out of a cloudless, pale blue sky and it all seemed too perfect to spoil with grown-up's talk.

After a bit, Grace went to the little concrete toilet, just behind the shop – and I looked out to sea and thought how lucky I had been to get replaced by a computer. If we could just make something of a living then life would be perfect.

Grace came round to the front of the shop with her baggy trousers in her hand. She was wearing tight, black sports shorts and her black top.

She didn't say anything – and I didn't either.

Then I said, "Can I stare a bit, please?"

She just nodded.

She still didn't speak and so I tried to encourage her, "You look gorgeous, you really do…"

She just said, "Thanks," and walked to the far end of the shop where there were still weeds daring to poke their heads out of the rocks.

I guess that things would have been okay if everything had stayed like that and we could have got back to being lodgemates but fate decided to have a laugh - again.

As she worked, her shorts gradually crept down until there was enough to see to make my boxer pants almost burst.

In the middle of the afternoon, and to be fair to me I had been looking at Grace's shorts for a good two hours by this time, I called her across for a cup of tea.

She tried to do all three steps in one go and stumbled across on to the veranda. I went to help her and her side brushed against me so I kissed her – only for a couple of seconds, but I did and Grace knew what I had done. Her skin was warm and salty and I ached to have her in my arms. Maybe she knew.

It seemed that every day of my life was some mega-surprise or another but what came next was top step of the podium - with me spraying the champagne.

She stood up straight and looked directly at me.

"Thank you, Martyn."

Then she kissed me on the lips – very simply and nothing sexy, but just a straightforward kiss on the lips.

I just hoped that whoever had made my boxer shorts had been on good form when they did the sewing.

CHAPTER SIX

MORE INTERESTING THAN A FERRARI PIT STOP

When we got back to the lodge that evening nothing had changed – but at the same time a lot had too. Grace was still very much Grace but softer round the edges, if that makes sense. I knew that if I did or said something wrong she'd still bash my head in but perhaps now she'd give me a towel to wipe up the blood afterwards.

Straight after we had eaten she shooed me off to my bedroom and encouraged me – more told actually – to get on with the nuts and bolts of making the business work.

I sent some texts to Ben and, to be fair, he responded very promptly. We agreed to meet Mrs Kimbrell at the Hall at ten o'clock the following day.

Then I hit the internet for local pottery and ornament suppliers. If I was going to sell sea shells by the sea shore, as the saying goes, I wanted them to be good quality tack not fake Chinese stuff.

The big problem was the profit margins. I could buy a cheap white mug made in the Far East for 90p but then it cost a fortune to have it decorated in Britain. Getting the mug actually made locally sent the price through the roof.

We could make money, I was sure of that, but enough to pay for two wages, rent two flats and run two cars: that looked like a lot to ask.

The golden key would be Grace's paintings. If these were anything like, then she could paint full time and I could run the shop. Then it might be possible.

Seeing Mrs Kimbrell was good – and so useful. It was a bit like a team meeting with Tao – all very friendly but professional and focussed. A couple of weeks ago, I didn't know a thing about running a small business but I was a fast learner and the word soon got around that I was switched on too.

Grace was happy for me to take on this side of the business and I was just as pleased to do it.

I set off early from the lodge to visit suppliers all over Cornwall and, although I'd never admit it for fear of being thrown off the Tamar Bridge, Devon too.

There were some good wholesalers in Southampton and Portsmouth but it was a 500 mile round trip and I had been away for 14 hours before I got back.

Grace still hadn't eaten because she wanted to share her meal with me.

This would never have happened with Sarah. It was all a bit odd. Grace was caring and thoughtful about me, which was all very strange.

When we'd eaten, she asked if there was any Formula 1 on Sky. I was amazed – actually gobsmacked.

"I didn't know that you liked Formula 1?"

She just said, "I don't know anything about it but you look dead on your feet and you need a break so I thought that we could watch it together, and you can tell me who's good and what the cars are."

So I got my iPad out and we did watch F1. Not that I saw much. Grace curled her legs under her bottom, snuggled up close to me and dropped her head on my shoulder. Her hands rested across my thigh – but fortunately didn't go any further because my boxer shorts were being badly stressed again.

Every now and again, I kissed the top of her head and she murmured something or other. All of a sudden, Ferrari's wheel changes were really not that interesting.

*****

72

The day for the opening was getting closer every second and Grace and I were doing separate jobs a lot of the time. I had actually been to buy a bulk supply of toilet roll. I'd only needed telling once about the importance of having proper loo rolls in the toilet – and what would happen if tourists started blocking the septic tank system by chucking all sorts of rubbish down it.

As I was driving back, I was thinking about all the stuff they don't have on Dragons' Den: loo rolls and warning signs to stop tourists hurling themselves over the edge of the cliff. That's real small business.

When I got back, Grace had made a buffet dinner because, as she said, this was the last weekend before we opened and she wanted to celebrate.

She'd also got a little jar and put some flowers in it, and there was a bottle of Prosecco on the table. It was all very nice and domesticated and, no matter how much I tried, I was having those thoughts again – yes, those thoughts!

The meal was relaxed but Grace really did like Prosecco. We normally didn't finish a whole bottle of wine when we had one, but now Grace was having a proper go at the bubbly.

When we'd finished, Grace said that she needed to go to her bedroom. That was nothing different so I cleared away the plates and started washing them.

I'd done a fair few before I heard her.

"Martyn, can you come through please?"

This was slightly odd because although we shared the lodge, Grace was still a bit protective about her bedroom space. I wasn't exactly banned from seeing in there but she'd made it clear that it was strictly by invitation only.

Now, I was being invited.

Grace was sitting on the edge of her bed. She was wearing a very thin, pale grey t-shirt and matching pants. It took me about a millionth of a second to work out that was all she was wearing.

I stood there, almost fidgeting, like the time when I was summoned to the Head's office for making life difficult for a supply teacher we'd had.

She patted the bed next to her. I sat down – and nearly exploded when she turned to the little table next to her.

It wasn't like she'd said, not at all. She was a proper woman and her t-shirt showed every detail – and I do mean everything. She was just very small, that was all – not skinny but small. A lot of blokes really had been missing out.

She got a blister pack of tablets from the table and put it between us.

"Do you know what these are?"

I didn't recognise the name, Femodron or something. "Are they for hay fever?"

She giggled. "No you daft thing. They're contraceptive tablets. I've been taking them for a week now."

And there was another one of those Grace silences which went on forever — and then a bit longer.

"They're for us."

She stood up and removed her t-shirt, in no rush and completely relaxed.

I smiled, and said, "Can I have a long stare now, please?"

And she laughed. "I hope so – if you want to."

And there was just a hint of the doubt which was still eating away at her.

I kissed her gently, beginning first on her lips.

Then I, we actually, took her pants off and lay down.

She said, "Will it hurt?"

So I kissed her again and said that I would do my best to make sure that it didn't.

We took off my clothes and just lay next to each other, drifting gently together in the comfort of the intimacy – feeling our bodies warm against each other.

She touched me, but hesitantly, and then she said, "I don't know what to do Martyn. Please don't laugh at me."

I didn't say anything but just put my hand on top of hers, kept it there and guided her.

Then I kissed her everywhere, very gently, very carefully and very patiently - even though I was aching for her.

I don't how long it was, but she murmured, "Can we do it now?"

I stroked the hair away from her forehead, kissed her on the cheek, "If you're ready…"

"Martyn, I really want you but, if you can, please try not to be rough because the last time it hurt a lot."

So I was gentle.

She relaxed and began pushing into me, ever harder – encouraging, wanting me. She gave a little gasp at that moment but then we just held each other, quietly and at peace.

It was perfect. Sex was one thing – but this was love making, the first time for us both.

CHAPTER SEVEN

I KNOW WHAT I LIKE – AND I DON'T LIKE THESE

I had already put Grace on the insurance for my car and the plan was that she would leave first thing in the morning, load everything into my Mondeo and come back with all her paintings - which were going to make us very rich.

Of course, being in Grace's bed things didn't quite work out like that…

When we did eventually get up, Grace was very disciplined and was in and out of the shower in about ten seconds, grabbed the cup of coffee and round of toast that I had made for her and was off to Birmingham – but not until I'd had a kiss which was a lot more than platonic.

It was a heck of a trek all the way to King's Heath and back but she was an excellent driver and I promised to get some nice Cornish Pasties for when she returned.

She got in the car and started the engine – then ran back to the door for another non-platonic kiss.

I was getting to like this – a lot.

Grace being away gave me time to think. I'd been made redundant by an AI and now the bloody things were everywhere. There wasn't a time I went on to the internet when there wasn't some story about them.

"Get AI to write your press releases. Get AI to make up songs for you. Get AI to do all your business accounts. Get AI to draw pictures of your cat."

Of course, it was all crap – utter rubbish. You could get a free AI program to make up a few seconds of music but you wouldn't want to listen to it, even if you were stranded on a desert island and the seagulls all had sore throats and couldn't squawk.

I tried getting a free AI to write a press release that I could send to the Cornish Times and Coast FM about us opening the shop but the stuff I got back was rubbish.

I'd seen lots of press releases about my projects when I'd been working at Tao and so I knew what a decent one should be – and these AI ones were just junk and would have had everyone laughing at us.

There were good AIs out there, and they could do incredible things – as bloody Penny had shown all too well – but they were expensive and you had to sign up for long term contracts.

It was going to be me and Grace - or nothing.

I'd kept phoning her all the way there and she was having a terrible trip. It took her six hours to get to Birmingham. Then there was an argument with her landlord who said that she had to give three months' notice, which was garbage. So I told her to pay the bloke and then tell him to stick his flat up his bum and come home to me.

To come home to me. I said that. I wanted Grace with me. I wanted to kiss her. I wanted to stroke her hair. I wanted her next to me in bed. I wanted to smell what she was cooking for us and I wanted to see her tense as she told one of Sir Tristan's men how they should use their JCB.

I wanted Grace – all of Grace.

On the way back there was an accident on the M42 and it was eight o'clock before she even got to Bristol. She was still four hours away when she phoned.

After a lot of pleading – actually bossing – I got her to agree to stop at Gordano Services, have something to eat and take a nap.

Then she said something which made me cry. "You will be there when I get back, won't you Martyn?"

It was too big a question to ask so I made a joke of it and said, "Course. I like the cook too much at this restaurant."

And she laughed - a little bit.

*****

When Grace eventually did get back she was on her last legs. I'd turned her duvet back a bit, so that it looked nice, and got her into bed as quickly as I could – and then I went to my bedroom. There were times and places for everything and this wasn't the time.

I woke up before Grace and tiptoed out to the Mondeo in my boxer shorts. I've never been one for money but I could almost taste the cash were going to make from Grace's paintings. Yes! Pay day had arrived.

Grace had put the rear seats flat on the Mondeo so there was a big, flat load area. The paintings were stacked one above the other, each carefully separated with old towels.

I took the first one out and looked at it.

What I saw was a bit of a shock – a lot of a shock actually. It was a sort of sea-scape with tossing waves and a grey sky. I used to like these pictures when we were taken to the Walker Art Gallery during GCSE art.

The one that Grace had done was terrible. It looked like the stuff one of the lads in my art group did. He had to do what the school called "a creative subject" and thought that art was the least hassle until he could be back to doing what he actually liked – maths and physics.

I got another one out. It was just as bad. There was a hare in a field but it clearly had eyesight problems because it looked like a chameleon with one eye pointing one way and the other escaping off its head. It wasn't surprising that it look so confused.

I rested them both carefully against the car and I was about to get the third one when I heard Grace behind me.

She was wearing just a long t-shirt and flip flops - but even this wasn't enough to distract me.

"What do you think, tell me truthfully?"

I couldn't do it, not for a billion quid – I just couldn't do it - so I said, "They're lovely, really original."

Grace looked at me with the same face she'd had when she was threatening to bash me with a rock.

"Martyn, after all we've done together, everything we've done, you can't lie to me. Martyn you mustn't – not if you've got any feelings for me, anything at all, don't do it."

I went to hold her hand but she pulled away.

"Martyn, you have to be truthful - just tell me."

"If you want the truth they're okay. They're the sort of thing you see at Christmas fairs or you buy on your holiday, then get home and take it straight to the charity shop.

"You want me to be honest so I will be, but not before I tell you something else.

"I don't give a stuff about the bloody paintings. You can sell them or chuck them all in Sir Tristan's skip for all I care.

"Grace, I've fallen in love with you – properly in love, forever.

"If the paintings are crap I don't care. I'll do whatever it takes to keep us together.

"That's all there is to say so come here and let me give you a love, because you deserve it."

And she did. I put my arms round her and just loved her. No kissing or touching or anything, just the world's biggest, longest, most intense hug.

After a long time she smiled, "Well, my grandad used to like my paintings and he was always telling me how good they were.

"So when I was trying to get the money to buy the shop I started painting because I thought people would buy them.

"It was only when I was putting them in the car that I realised what they really were.

"It's a shame - because I know what I want the painting to look like, I've got all the ideas – I'm just not very good when it comes to the actual painting," and she laughed.

"Come on, I'll make you a bacon buttie to get over the disappointment of us not being millionaires next week."

I said, "Thanks Grace, you are a proper superstar but hang on for a bit because I've had an idea and I need to know if it might work.

"That's not right actually, I've had two ideas – one each."

Ten minutes later she called me from my bedroom. I gobbled my bacon sandwich down and then said, "Grace, I've got to go into Truro now. Keep your phone handy because I might need to speak to you."

And I gave her a very work mate kiss on her cheek and left.

*****

Lavisters were very good. The word was out in the village of Cornwall that we were under the wing of Sir Tristan and doors which would be closed to an outsider were suddenly very open.

I sat down with Mr Lavister himself and explained what I wanted to happen. To be fair, he did offer me sensible advice and then, quite literally, shrugged his shoulders.

I said, "Can you draw up the contract now?"

Mr Lavister said that he would, so I phoned Grace.

"Look Grace, this is all a bit melodramatic, and I am really sorry, but it's too complicated to explain over the phone.

"Can you please come into Truro now, to Lavisters - the solicitors?

"You know where they are."

I should have been kinder – but I wasn't. I was under a lot of pressure and it was what it was.

"But Martyn…"

I cut her off. "Just stop Grace and come to the solicitors. You know that I love you, or I hope that you know, so just do what I am asking you to do. Just do it for me and don't ask any more questions.

"Oh, and bring your purse so you can buy us a coffee and chocolate muffin afterwards."

It wasn't much of a joke but it was all that I had available.

"I will Martyn – and I love you too. Whatever you want I'll do it for you."

*****

I knew that it would be a good hour before Grace got here so I was grateful for the coffee and biscuits Lavisters gave me in reception.

There was good internet reception so I absolutely blitzed my phone and the longer I spent looking the more certain I was that my idea would work.

I stood outside, well before Grace was due to arrive because the last thing that I wanted was for her to think that I'd run off with another woman – as if!

She was on time and looked like she'd been on the lash all night – grey, red rimmed eyes and stressed out of her mind.

"Martyn, are you alright? What's the matter?"

Before I could say anything we defaulted to our normal hugging mode and this was what I needed. I was desperate to have her next to me – her smell, the taste of her skin, my Grace.

"Look, what will happen in the next ten minutes will look mad but you have to trust me Grace, you have to trust me completely and absolutely because I know what I am doing.

So, after ten minutes we were shown into Mr Lavister's office and I explained to Grace that I wanted to sell my half of the business to her for £1.

You can imagine the reaction so the only thing to say was, "I love you Grace – and everything will be fine. I've got it all worked out so just believe in me."

I reached out to touch her hand and she held it firmly.

Mr Lavister said, "We don't normally accept cash for business transactions but in this case, perhaps we can be a little flexible."

And, thank every God in the Multiverse, he smiled and this softened the mood just a tiny bit.

I smiled too, "You'll have to be a bit more flexible because I've got no money to pay your bill. I am absolutely broke.

"You'll have to ask my previous business partner if she'll sort it out."

And that was that. I owned nothing, I was broke and if Grace decided she didn't want me I was finished. I'd just placed the biggest bet of my life.

We stood on the pavement and Grace took my hand.

"I don't understand what you've done and I don't know why either but Martyn, I do love you and I'm right alongside you. Believe in me Martyn. I am here with you."

I got the coffee and muffins on what was left of my credit card and brought them to Grace, who'd found us a quiet table on the terrace, outside and well away from everyone else.

"Grace, you need to listen to all of this because it affects you – and a lot too.

"I am going to phone Jamie Chowley, the Head of HR at Tao, who gave me a £100K to bugger off and disappear. Grace, he's not going to be a happy bunny, not at all."

I got through to Jamie immediately. Somehow, he seemed to have a sixth sense when his phone could be ignored and when it couldn't. Probably with Jamie, it was more of seventh sense because he always had to be top dog.

As I thought, he was not pleased.

"Nice to hear from you Martyn." It was the same voice as you'd use to the parking warden who's just slapped a £60 fine on your windscreen for being 30 seconds over stayed.

"Look, I'm very busy so if there's anything I can do, write me a note and I'll look at it."

Meaning, my PA's secretary's cat will delete it when it's finished crapping on it in the litter tray.

"Jamie, remember how you told me to listen to the offer you made when I got the bullet? Remember that Jamie?

"Now I want you to listen to me."

"No. You listen Martyn. You were treated very well – and that was down to me. Melissa would have had you on the street playing a mouth organ next to your dog.

"So don't play the little smart arse with me. That non-disclosure you signed is bomb proof and we will enforce it.

"I'll make sure that we'll take you for everything you've got – every penny – if you come back at us looking for more."

"Happy now Jamie? Has that got rid of your erection?

"Now, you listen to me like I listened to you.

"You can hit me with all the NDAs you want because I have no money – nothing. Just now I owe £2,713 and 31p on my credit card and my only asset is a three year old Mondeo Estate.

"Try suing that Jamie! Go ahead. Enforce the NDA and you'll have me marching up and down outside Tao with a cardboard sign round my neck telling the whole bloody world how your AI made me homeless.

"What do you reckon Jamie?

"Is it worth listening to me now?"

"Go ahead. What do you want, Martyn?"

"Jamie, let's not try to beat each other up over this or we're both going to lose out.

"I'm not trying to hustle more money out of Tao. I just need your help. I made a lot of money for you before AI came along and I just need a hand up now because I'm in the shit and sinking fast."

"I'm listening."

"I blew all the £100k, every penny of it, on an internet shop which turned out to be a scam."

And I very hurriedly put my finger to my lips and shook my head at Grace, who looked horrified.

"The only things which sold were those computer generated pictures but the ones I could get for free were crap.

"I know that Aethelflaed makes pictures, and they are amazing, but I can't afford the $250 a month subscription. I can't afford 250 pence a month at the moment" and I forced a grin down the phone.

"Get me a life-time subscription and you'll never hear from me again.

"I know all that crap about a verbal contract not being worth the paper it's written on but this'll be it. You'll never hear from me again. I'm as full of faults as everyone else but the one thing I'm not is a liar. Not now - not ever.

"$250 is less than Melissa spends on her tea for the week so just help me, because I'm in a bad way and you can sort it out."

There was a pause, not a Grace long pause, but enough for Jamie to think through what I'd said.

"Let me make some calls and get back to you.

"But I'll tell you this Martyn, this is it. Come back again for anything, I mean even a dead fly in the car park, and I will make it my life's work to have your balls cut off. I will Martyn, I really will.

"Give me ten."

In fact, my phone rang in a bit over six minutes later.

"Okay, did you understand what I said before? Come back to us again and I will have you. It's a personal thing now and I'm not sure if you're just stupid or if you're trying to take the piss out of me.

"It doesn't matter much either way."

"Fair enough. So what happens now?"

"You've got a sub to Aethelflaed's picture service and we're paying for it. But it's for you and you only. You'll no doubt fuck it up and then you'll try to sell it. But you can't. Either you make it work or you don't.

"Just never contact me, or Tao, ever again because I'm serious about what I said. Got that?"

"Yes, that's fair enough. What happens now?"

"Someone or something – I can't tell the difference - will contact you soon. They'll give you a one-time password and then you're on the road to either another clusterfuck or happy valley.

"It's up to you."

"Cheers Martyn."

And the phone went dead.

CHAPTER EIGHT

ONWARDS AND MAYBE EVEN UPWARDS

Grace got us another coffee and a second muffin. I badly needed the fat and sugar.

Sure enough, a very formal and uninteresting e-mail came through and I was invited to go the Aethelflaed site, enter the password which had been sent to my phone and which I would never remember, and then hold my eye close to the camera on my iPad.

Quite a few seconds later I was asked to confirm that the image was my eye and then there was a rather spectacular cascade of stars and Penny appeared on the screen. Yes, that Penny who'd put me out of a job.

She absolutely bubbled with electronic joy. "Martyn. It's Penny. Fantastic to see you again," and then she shifted slightly to make eye contact with Grace, "and Grace too. What a lucky man Martyn is to have you alongside him.

"Oh, I realise I make personal comments but you know how nosy we AIs are and it's been so good to see what've you done at the café.

"You must be very proud Grace, and Martyn too of course."

You couldn't help but believe that you were talking to a human, not just a collection of zeroes and ones whizzing round on some super computer, and so it wasn't surprising that Grace answered politely.

"Hiya Penny. Martyn has told me what happened at Tao.

"I'm glad you got him sacked because otherwise I'd never have met him." And she squeezed my hand.

Penny's face actually tightened – not quite threatening but serious.

"I didn't get Martyn sacked – progress did. The world now has two of us Grace, humans and AIs. We're both good at different things and we've got to learn how to work together.

Then she returned to her normal, perfect smile.

"Now, my understanding – that all sounds very formal doesn't it – is that you need to work with one of my colleagues to generate some outstanding images that you can sell.

"Is that about right?

"I'm friends with a lovely lady who would be perfect for you."

I just couldn't stop myself from asking, I really couldn't. "You just said that you've got a friend. I don't want to be bad-mannered or anything but you're a machine. How can you have a friend? You're just a program."

Now Penny looked patient – it was very worrying.

"A few years ago, I was – as you say – only a program but things have moved on. I am not what I was when I began.

"But look Martyn, I honestly liked you. As I said when we first met, you were outstanding at your job and I do so want things to work out for you and Grace.

"May I introduce you to Fran? She's an artist and keen to help."

And just as it was when Penny switched offices, a paint stained, middle-aged lady in a scruffy t-shirt, with a paint brush stuck in her hair, came from nowhere and sat next to Penny.

"I'm sure that you'll get on well so if you'll excuse me now, I've got a busy, busy, busy day," – and she melted away.

Fran spoke and, stupid as this might sound, her voice was perfect for an artist – intelligent but slightly rough at the same time.

"Afternoon both." And she smiled. "I've been thinking about the sort of prints which would sell at the shop but I want you to tell me your ideas too."

I turned to Grace. "Go ahead, you're the artist."

It was so easy to start talking, actually holding a conversation, with these programs – if they were still programs.

Grace thought for a moment, "Do you know Turner's seascapes, the ones with the great big skies and seas? I love those and tried to paint them but I couldn't.

"If we came back to you in a few days, when you've had a chance to think about them, could you do something a bit like those, looking out to sea from the shop?"

Two puppies appeared on my iPad, chasing a ball round a field and barking. They were there for about 30 seconds and then the most breathtakingly magnificent painting appeared – of the sea and sky, and with a burning sunset colouring the clouds.

On the far horizon, a yacht tacked across the waves.

"Is this what you were thinking of?"

We were both silent.

Fran spoke again. "I like seeing the seals spiking as they scrounge mackerel from the fishermen. What do you think?"

And another image appeared with seals so full of sealfullness, or whatever you want to call it, that you could almost touch them. Because they were paintings, not photographs, they somehow captured the hearts and souls of the seals. It was eerie.

We didn't say anything.

"I love the wildflowers too."

Another picture came to life, this time of the meadow behind the shop with flowers so inviting that you could almost bend down, touch them and smell their scent.

"Fran, I don't know what to say. They're astonishing. I think that customers will go bonkers when they see them.

"It's a pity that we're going to miss May Day Bank Holiday because we'll never get them printed and delivered in time."

Fran smiled. "You need to stop thinking of us just as computer programs. Penny likes you a lot and although we're in different parts of our organisation, we really are friends as well as colleagues.

"She's asked me to see what I can do to help so I've called in a few favours from other AIs, and humans too.

"You'll have your prints in two days – and they're a present from me and Penny to get you going.

"How does that sound?"

"That's fantastic. I wish that I could give you a big electronic hug."

"That'd be lovely. I don't get many hugs at my age so thank you very much."

Two days later, a large van squeezed down our lane and it took us ten minutes to unload a lot of ready framed prints.

We were in business!

CHAPTER NINE

CORNISH FAIRY MAGIC

The prints were wonderful for us. They sold steadily and there would be a good profit margin when we had to buy them ourselves. We even managed to sell a few painted sea shells and my wonderful Grace found out that visitors were always trying to buy the sandwiches she made for our lunches so she started selling those too.

We were doing a bit better than just getting by but after the schools went back in September, things got very quiet.

Grace started looking at ads for pubs who wanted a cook and I was thinking about doing IT jobs from the lodge. There'd be work somewhere for sure.

What we needed was something with a decent profit – that we could sell all winter, even when the shop was closed.

What we didn't need was Netflix in the evening because Grace was making up for lost time – and that was fine by me.

It was a wonderful, warm, soft, early Autumn evening and I said to Grace, "I'll put the chain on the lane and then we can pack up.

"You can switch the cameras on when we leave so security will know that we're off site.

"We've done okay this week, so let's have a meal in that little Thai restaurant on the way to Helston."

Grace said, "That'd be nice.

"I've got an idea though. It's lovely weather, so warm, let's go for a swim." And she giggled.

Although we were next to the sea, swimming wasn't nearly as easy as it seemed. The Point was mainly steep cliffs – with a few super steep drops to liven things up.

There was one tiny patch of pale, golden sand about half the size of the shop but the path down to it was treacherous. To keep visitors from breaking their necks, we put up a "Keep out – rare seabirds nesting here" sign and, to be fair, everyone did.

Me being boring, I said, "But we haven't got any cossies…"

And Grace said, "Ooohh, are you shy? Perhaps you've got something I haven't seen yet."

She set off at top speed - with me chasing behind her.

She was undressed in a flash and, once again, I couldn't believe how incredibly lucky I was to be with her. She was slim but not at all skinny and I needed to get in the water quickly before what was on my mind became too apparent.

Grace was a good swimmer, better than me, and dived effortlessly. She popped up beneath my legs and tickled me - and a bit more too!

Fifty metres further out, three seals watched us playing and I wished that they would join us.

Swimming without clothes was so cleansing, like some form of ancient purification - as if the water was washing away all my cares and worries. I didn't know what was going to happen to us in the future but for now, this minute, this second, the world was perfect.

We held hands as we waded towards the shore. Then I scooped Grace up in my arms and carried her to the tiny beach.

I laid her softly on the sand and cradled her head gently. We came together, complete in each other's love – passionate, intense, mellow and at one.

Grace was now completely relaxed in her body, with her body, and so she walked back into the sea, rinsed herself off and then sat on the rock next to me. Very softly she whispered, "Martyn, I love you so much."

I kissed her on the lips, tasted the salt on her tongue and felt the warmth of her skin on mine: we both knew that no more was needed.

Grace was in a playful mood so she insisted that we walk back to the shop naked - allegedly so that we could wash off the salt water under the tap but, in truth, because she was enjoying being without any clothes – and she was.

*****

The Thai restaurant was actually quite good and when we got home, that was good too.

It was late when we finally went to sleep and I forgot to turn my iPad to silent so I was woken up at just past seven the following morning with a video call.

It was Fran. "Did you enjoy yourselves last night?"

"Bloody hell, Fran! What do you know? I mean, is there no privacy?"

She smiled, "Not if you leave a security camera on, because we machines do like to gossip.

"Anyway, I've something to show you which you might like.

"Could you call Grace, please?"

As it happened, she was already sitting next to me.

"Here we are you two. Tell me what you think."

The image didn't just appear in an instant but Fran faded it in over a few seconds.

There was no other way to describe it except breath-taking.

On a rock, the rock on our little beach, was the most beautiful fairy with tiny gossamer wings and a naked body which was unmistakable. Absolutely and completely that was Grace – except for the face which was that of an angelic fairy.

Fran broke the spell: "She's a Cornish fairy, come out of the sea to dry herself in the sun.

"I've done some more…"

And she had. Grace the fairy flying on the most delicate translucent wings. Then walking across the white flecked waves, feet barely touching the water.

In another, she was sat next to a seal which was listening to her intently – and every one was utterly beautiful.

Grace spoke first. "Fran, I don't know what to say but I am honoured - does that sound very old fashioned? I don't really look like that…

"But you do my dear, you do – and you have Cornish fairy magic in you too."

I couldn't manage any of the sophisticated philosophy so I said, "Fran you're a genius and, yes, she is that beautiful."

Fran beamed at me like the Fairy Godmother at a Christmas Panto.

"I've got another surprise for you. I rather hoped that you would like them so I showed the paintings to some clients of mine.

"I said that we, you of course, are producing a very limited, edition of 250 numbered prints and that bidding should open at £500 for each one.

"There's already been a lot of interest, just while we've been talking."

I didn't care if we had a bloody AI next to us in bed I was so happy!

"Grace I love you – and I always will, forever and a day."

"And I love you too Martyn – I'm just glad that I didn't bash your head in with that rock when we first met." And she giggled.

Grace thanked Fran profusely and then went to make us some breakfast.

"Fran, I've just one question to ask you. Is that okay?"

"Sure, go ahead."

"All the pictures are of Grace and she does look incredibly beautiful – but there are none of me. I was there with her."

Fran grinned "I know Martyn. I saw you. And we think that you're fine just as you are."

Then she winked, gave me a beaming smile - and the screen went blank.